'Bye, Captain,' the figure said, and threw the emergency handle on the outer door.

A square of black space and stars was suddenly rushing towards James at frightening speed, and hard needles probed his ears. There was blood on his nose and chin, and droplets were spraying off in a blue-red shower as the air funnelled past and out into vacuum at high speed. Something hard and sharp stung the palm of his right hand, and he grabbed it before he had slid on past. He tried to shout, but the words were torn from his mouth; and now, as the thin cable began to slide through the flesh of his hand, he felt his one hold on safety going. He had a blurred, inverted view of the crewroom, torn papers and all the detritus of a working area swirling down towards the open door and spouting into free vacuum; then the meat was ripped from the palm of his hand in an instant of raw pain and the blackness and stars yawned and swallowed him.

# Saturn Three

A novelisation by
Steve Gallagher from
the film screenplay

SPHERE BOOKS LIMITED
30/32 Gray's Inn Road, London WC1X 8JL

First published in Great Britain by Sphere Books Ltd. 1980
Novelisation copyright © Sphere Books 1980
Saturn Three copyright © MCMLXXX ITC Entertainment Ltd.
All Rights Reserved

TRADE
MARK

Set in Monotype Plantin

Printed in Great Britain by
William Collins Sons & Co Ltd
Glasgow

# ONE

The base on Tethys, third moon of Saturn, was considered by most of the academics who formed the policies of the Saturn Survey Team to be the least promising of its research stations. Titan – now, that was another matter. Saturn's first and biggest moon had promise, prestige, even an atmosphere of sorts; not that the sluggish mantle of methane and ammonia vapour was much of a reminder of the thin and acrid breathing mixture of home, but it was possible for those who worked on Saturn Six to delude themselves that their work had planetary research status. Tethys, though – Tethys was no more than a snowball, a six-hundred mile chunk of ammonia ice and grit. Even Saturn Five on Rhea was considered a better prospect than Tethys, and Rhea was generally acknowledged to be the Spacers' graveyard.

Those who took the Orion shuttle to the massive Saturn orbiting platform came either to make the transfer to Titan or to study the masses of data continuously radioed in from Saturn Six. In fact, so Titan-oriented had the Saturn Survey become that the orbit of the platform had been shifted to give more or less unbroken communication with the base; this was hard luck for Rhea and Tethys, where Five and Three sometimes had to endure long periods of planetary eclipse without contact or support, but as the range of experiments and the promise of Saturn Six grew no sleep was lost over the problems of the minor bases. Their workload and personnel were cut in roughly equal proportions, leaving the buried complexes as little more

5

than perfunctory scientific outposts, dispirited watch-towers in a cold and blasted corner of the solar system.

If an evaluation were to be made on a purely scientific basis Tethys might, in many ways, score far higher than Titan; if the purposes of the experimentation programmes were solely those set out in the survey prospectus – that is, the discovery of a means whereby the fixed nitrogen locked in the ammonia around Saturn could be processed into a viable growth medium for food organisms, and the methane provide a base for a bacterial protein culture – if these considerations were the only ones with a real importance attached to them the focus of research energy would probably have been on Saturn Three. Unfortunately such purity of purpose is rarely a feature of professional science, concerned as it so often is with an egotistical contest for the recognition of posterity; and so the extensive gas resources of Tethys were ignored in favour of the cold and difficult fogs of Titan.

Adam wasn't worried. Far from being a place of exile, Tethys was to him a corner of quiet sanity, a retreat from a brutal and self-obsessed society. He welcomed each successive withdrawal of contact, and breathed a quiet sigh each time the satellite's spectacular primary interposed itself between his station antenna and the continuous harsh jargon of the broadcasting platform. The trouble with the rat race, he maintained, was that the rats had too much of an advantage. They won every time. If this isolation was the price he would have to pay to retain his humanity, he would go on paying it gladly.

And, of course, there was Alex Alexandra, the most gracious and elegant name he'd been able to think of when he'd found she had none of her own, only the unattractive serial number that was the reference code of the space-born. At first the storybook-city name had been his own private tag, a mental label that he found himself using whenever he thought of this young stranger with whom he'd come to share his posting; but then, as the easy familiarity of close contact grew, Adam had told her of this frivolous conceit. Far from being amused, as he'd feared, she accepted the name as if it had been a personal gift, and from that point onwards their personal lives had merged to the same degree as their professional duties. Adam was wary of this, although he did nothing to resist the process – although in the best condition of a hardened spacer he was much older than she, and it depressed him to suspect that Alex's affection might be directed towards him not because he alone could command it, but because he alone was available to receive it.

If Alex ever gave the matter any thought, she didn't show it. Once the initial barriers of personal distance had been crossed she demonstrated a distinct lack of inhibition in their relationship, as if she recognised his reserve and was determined to compensate for it. The night that she'd moved in with him was still fresh in Adam's mind; there had been a knock on the sliding door to his quarters, and as a joke he'd called out 'Who is it?' When he opened the door Alex was standing there in a loose shirt and holding an armload of rumpled bedding.

'My dorm warden threw me out,' she said with an undisguisable mischief in her eyes. 'Can I stay with you for a few days until I find a new place?'

Adam's insecurity had weathered under her attention. Now, as he accelerated the surface buggy towards the ridge that would mark the start of the last stretch of the drive home, he could feel that it was beginning to return. Their last communication from the platform had contained news of an impending visit; the message had been more eloquent in its omissions than it had been informative in its statements. He hadn't yet told Alex about it. No doubt she would be excited by this variation in the routine of the base, and he felt a twinge of guilt for keeping this simple pleasure from her. He would tell her as soon as he got back and had unloaded the samples from the buggy.

The rugged vehicle chewed its way up the last few yards of broken ground and lurched over the ridge, its sprung body flexing in the middle to cope with the sudden change in the terrain. One of the rear wheels spun loose for a moment before the axle dropped and the coiled metal tyres got a new bite on the sloping ice-rock. Black crystals glittered and showered slowly down in the low gravity behind the buggy as Adam increased the hydrogen burn to speed him home. Ahead stretched the tracks of innumerable expeditions like this one, ranging wide but all converging on the unimpressive hump of plated metal that was the uncovered upper level of Saturn Three. Beyond this was a low and jagged horizon only a few miles distant, a toothed black saw which cut into the awesome vista beyond; for Tethys's airless sky was filled with the yellow belted splendour of Saturn, an angled halo of light brilliantly defining the curvature of space about the gas giant.

The buggy skipped and bucketed down the slope, cutting fresh tracks in silence. Of course he would tell Alex. Perhaps later.

# TWO

Captain James awoke with a start, jerked from his sleep by an inexplicable feeling of urgency. For a moment he stared, uncomprehending, into the darkness; the familiar shapes of his cabin furniture loomed in dim outline, picked out by the soft blue night-glow of the wall lighting panels. As these few details sketched themselves into his mind he began to relax, and the mild panic that he had felt upon awakening was replaced by a curiosity as to why this should be his reaction. Nerves, perhaps; his first solo drop as a full captain-handler was due to take place this shift, but then he had always prided himself on a professional coolness which rarely allowed such bursts of uncontrolled fever.

He pushed the thin sheets back and reached for the bedside switch to bring the cabin to life. No point waiting for the preset to do it for him, now that he was already awake; as the glow of the panels increased and the coffee spigot made a welcome gurgling sound into the cup he levered himself up in the narrow bunk and half-rolled to get a look at the bedside timer.

James blinked a couple of times, but the red-etched figures on the timer's face didn't alter. Surely there was some fault with the display . . that *couldn't* be right . . .

The protestations of his reason were cut short by a shrill tone that broke in suddenly from the com point panel let into the wall above the timer. He reached out and touched the marked square that would open the channel, swinging his legs out of the bunk as he did so and lurching to his feet.

'Captain James?' The voice from the com point

managed to make the rank sound like a mild reprimand.

'Yes. Speaking.'

'Launch three nine two, sir. Your drop to Saturn Three, Tethys base. We've got a ship and we've got most of a cargo – all we need now is a pilot.'

James had his locker open, was scrambling through the clothes on the rail to find his drop undersuit. 'I'm on my way,' he called over his shoulder.

'We're at commit minus fifteen,' the crewman at launch control said. 'If you don't make it we'll have to abort.'

'I said I'm on my way!' Where the hell was the drop suit? He had a spare, but that didn't carry his new rank flashes. The crewman cut the link from his end, but not before he'd let the microphone pick up a pointed sign of resignation.

James tried to pull the spare suit out of the locker. His other clothes tangled around it and he felt a growing and uncontrollable frustration beginning to rob his movements of their usual economy. He gave a hard yank and dragged the suit free, throwing it across the bunk in an angry gesture. Two of his shirts slid from their hangers and dropped in a heap to the bottom of the locker but he ignored them, bounding the door shut and turning to move to the bathroom cubicle.

Splashing a double handful of cold water on to his face, he told himself to be calm. Fifteen minutes was sufficient time to get to the crewroom on the platform's outer skin and suit himself up for the drop. He'd done it often enough as second man on the shuttle, and there was no reason why the preparations for this first solo should take him any longer. What he couldn't understand was his oversleeping; he could remember setting the room's timer to wake him with more than an hour to spare before the drop. He was wide awake when he did it, because it had been just before Benson and Mazursky had called in to shake his hand and offer their best wishes on his completion of the course. All the lights had been on, and he was sure he hadn't made a mistake. So why had it been left to his inner clock to snap him awake with only fifteen minutes to prepare?

No time to worry about it now, any more than he could afford to go on digging through his locker to find his undersuit. He dropped on to the bed and started pulling on the spare; it annoyed him to have to go on his first solo with only Captain's flashes on his shoulders, but he didn't have much choice. The com point started to warble again as he moved to leave the room, but he ignored it – he could be polite or he could be on time, but not both.

He slapped his breast pocket as he stepped into the curved central corridor of the officers' quarters, reassured to feel the hard shape of his duplicate crewroom locker key under the zippered flap. He began to jog towards the central concourse and the elevators· that would take him to the outer skin of the orbiting platform, and as his running moved into an even rhythm he felt his control returning. He would be in the crewroom in three minutes, four at the most. Two minutes to step into his pressure suit and slap across the self-locking seals, and a couple more to walk through to the launch bay airlock, fixing the seals on his helmet as he went . . . he'd do it with no problem.

Don't forget the braincase, he reminded himself as he pushed his way through a crowd of new arrivals from the Orion shuttle. You'd look a damn fool arriving at Saturn Three with a new Demigod robot and no brain-case to put in it. Some of the people looked at him with undisguised interest as he stepped into the elevator and touched the square for the launch bay level; his assured haste marked him out as a professional, a man of action. He allowed himself to savour the feeling as the elevator made its fast 'descent' to the outer shell of the rotating station, but was pulled out of his brief reverie of self-admiration as the doors opened and he heard his name over the utilities area public address system.

'Captain James for launch three nine two. We are nearing abort status on this launch unless we get your presence, Captain.'

James pulled the crewroom door open and stepped over the threshold. It was a bulkhead pressure door with a quarter-turn wheel at its centre, an essential safety measure as the crewroom was right on the outer skin and had a direct-exit door at its far end which could be blown in a launch bay emergency. At this moment, however, the ponderous steel portal was more of an obstacle than a salvation. He was being paged on the tannoy like some inexperienced space monkey, and it irritated him.

Automatics took over and pulled the pressure door closed as James moved down the central suspension catwalk to his locker. Somebody else was at the far end of the catwalk, already suited and anonymous, and James raised a hand in half-greeting. This wasn't a time to get involved in a conversation. The suited figure straightened a little from whatever it was he was doing, and acknowledged James's wave.

James palmed the narrow identifying strip of foil and held it level with the sensor on the locker as he tapped in the combination. As the door swung open he pocketed the key and reached inside for his pressure suit.

He stepped into the legs of the suit and closed the seals, and then as they bound and locked reached deeper into the locker and brought out a tall cylinder of brushed metal. There was an indicator dial on the top and he wasted a few precious seconds in checking it; temperature variations could be fatal to nitrogen-cooled brain-cases. All was fine. He turned to pull on the arms and gloves of the suit.

Something was wrong. The tailored glove didn't slide easily on to his hand as it should; the fingers were too short and the wrist was too wide. Somewhere outside the tannoy was calling for him again, muffled by the curving bulkhead walls but still recognisable – and he couldn't move because suddenly his suit wouldn't fit.

It was Benson's suit, that was why.

Benson's tag was inside the chest flap, and the flashes on the suit's shoulders were for sub-Captain's rank like the outdated ones on James's own lightweight undersuit. So how did Benson's pressure suit come to be in James's locker? And where the hell was James's own suit?'

There was a crackle from the suit intercom of the figure at the end of the catwalk. James looked up at the noise, frowning in perplexity.

'Bye, Captain,' the figure said, and threw the emergency handle on the outer door.

A square of black space and stars was suddenly rushing towards James at frightening speed, and hard needles probed his ears. There was blood on his nose and chin, and droplets were spraying off in a blue-red shower as the air funnelled past and out into vacuum at high speed. Something hard and sharp stung the palm of his right hand, and he grabbed it before he had slid on past. It was one of the twisted wire cables which supported the catwalk and it gave him enough grip to pull him up so that he bobbed helpless in the fierce airstream. He tried to shout, but the words were torn from his mouth; and now, as the thin cable began to bite through the flesh of his hand, he felt his one hold on safety going. He had a blurred, inverted view of the crewroom, torn papers and all the odd detritus of a working area swirling down towards the open door and spouting into free vacuum, and that single suited figure pressed against the bulkhead for safety; then the meat was ripped from the palm of his hand in an instant of raw pain and the blackness and stars yawned and swallowed him.

It had taken no more than a few seconds for the sealed crewroom to belch its atmosphere out into space. The irresistible hurricane dropped as quickly as it had begun, and the man in the suit with the newly applied handler's flashes was able to lever himself away from the wall and turn the handle to close the outer door. As the chamber resealed itself he reached into the red box mounted on the wall beside him and re-cued the alarms that would sound a warning if the door should ever be inadvertently blown.

Air was easing back into the crewroom as he bent over the braincase canister. It had wedged in the locker and suffered no damage. He lifted it and set off for the launch bay.

Three minutes, and Launch three nine two would reach the stage where abandonment would be inevitable. Unbalanced slightly by the weight of the metal cylinder the Captain-handler passed through the high-speed vacuum locks and emerged into the cavernous launch bay. A number of helmets swung to bear on him, cumbersome and anonymous like armour; one man gave a jerky, impatient wave, and the Captain signed an apology.

If questions were to be asked, it would seem obvious that it was Benson who had spaced himself in a moment of black self-pity. If, by some remote chance, a body should be recovered – remote indeed, unless it fell into a trackable orbit – it would have Benson's suit and Benson's tags for identification. Obvious conclusions would be drawn from Benson's failure in the courses of skills that were a prerequisite of promotion, and from the diagnosis of potential instability that the series of response-control tests had thrown up. Benson was top-grade scrapheap as far as Saturn Survey was concerned, and the stigmata of his failures would follow him back to Earth. He'd be lucky if he could even get a parenthood licence. He'd probably done everyone a favour when he'd taken the jump. Captain James would be unconnected with the whole affair – after all, hadn't he gone and got himself buried on Tethys, teaching some robot to walk?

The service lines were already being withdrawn from the small spacecraft when he reached it and swung up the short ladder to the cockpit. He put the braincase carefully through the hatch ahead of him and then followed it, turning awkwardly in the confined space of the craft's interior to get to the command couch. The parts and systems that would make up the Demigod's body were already loaded and secured but the blank, unrecorded braincase was the handler's sole responsibility – quite appropriate when one considered the intimacy of contact that would be necessary during the period of the Demigod's education.

The bay doors were dropping, isolating the pad from the rest of the Saturn platform. The Captain chinned the switch in his helmet to open up his suit radio, and his head was instantly filled with the jargon and gabble of crosstalk. Somebody was wishing him a pleasant trip, but he didn't respond; they would probably be cursing his lateness as soon as he was out of range.

Launch bay lights went from white to red, and then began to flash warning as the countdown reached thirty seconds. Somewhere overhead the iris of the pad's accelerator tunnel was opening, ready to receive the spacecraft and fling it with the predetermined accuracy of an O'Neill mass driver into a planetary orbit which would intersect Saturn's 'A' ring and emerge into the moon-cleared Cassini division for rendezvous with Tethys on the far side of the primary.

The countdown reached zero, and a number of the switches on the craft's control board flared green. He touched them in order, each light dying as his gloved finger brushed the etched glass; the fingers of the suit were a little too long for comfort, but he could live with it. The craft responded to the sequence by beginning its burn, a deep-felt tug and an illusory increase in weight as the pad dropped from below and the influence of the accelerator rings began to take hold from above; and then the Captain was suddenly slapped back in the command couch, speeding headlong down the tunnel and then out into free space and on to his own directional power.

The sense of extreme forward motion was lost as the craft dropped away from the platform and moved towards a close orbit. There were no immediate points of reference here, and the universe became slow, bright and graceful to the observer. The craft was moving nearly parallel to the plane of the rings and it was almost possible to see them as a broad, solid highway of light, smooth and impenetrable; three uneven bands of reflective ice and dust, delineated with neat precision by the sweeping effect of Mimas, Enceladus and Tethys.

Tethys would be a good place to get buried for a while.

# THREE

Adam had told Alex about the impending visit less than
an hour after his return with the samples in the buggy.
As expected, she'd glowed at the change in routine, but
then Adam was pleased to see that she began to share his
trepidation without any prompting.

'Help?' she said. 'They've left us little enough to do.
Why should we need help?'

'I don't know,' said Adam, sincere in his ignorance.
'Some kind of robot is all they told me.'

'We already have robots. We don't need another.'

'This one's supposed to be special. Given time and
training . . .'

'Training? A robot?'

Adam shrugged. 'I only know what they told me.'

He couldn't bring himself to tell her the rest; not yet,
anyway. That this new class of robot, with time and
training, might eventually take over the duties of a
human being . . . or two. And that a reposting on the
Survey was unlikely to see them staying together; the
Survey's policy computer took no account of personal
attachments, and Adam understood that such practices
were out of fashion elsewhere in the system, anyway.

But there was no point in worrying her without cause.
In Adam's experience, the introduction of new technology invariably created work and worry rather than
abolished it; and a little more activity to fill the peaceful,
empty days wouldn't be unwelcome. And if Alex
wanted to be alarmed at a possible separation it should
be a spontaneous reaction, not one taken on cue from
him; he valued her happiness more than his own, and
he wouldn't want a sense of youthful duty towards him

to overcome and stifle it. Perhaps it was unfair to expect her to go on sharing this empty base with a much older man, cramping and curtailing her experience of life outside – but when he came to remember that life, his doubts dissolved and his fears subsided.

When radio silence was broken by a reflected echo from the station's own beacon they suited up and went to watch the landing. Adam had wanted to opt for caution, watching the spacecraft's descent on one of the screens in the communications room, but this had obviously so disappointed Alex that he had relented and agreed that they should watch from the comparative safety of the outer hangar. It was a large opening and would give them a good view, and it had the added advantage that it could be slammed shut at emergency speed if there was any danger from the spacecraft's approach.

The craft overshot at first, making a full loop around the diminutive moon to come storming in again from the far horizon, swinging around as it dropped towards the base and lining up its landing legs. The pilot obviously knew about Tethys's unusual composition because he cut the hot drives before they could brush the surface of the ground and bounced down the last few feet under the moon's gentle pull. Even so, the locked gases began to boil and swirl, but they re-liquified almost instantly and hardened into a brittle crust around the settled craft.

Adam and Alex moved forward from the hangar, two anonymous and indistinguishable figures in protective suits welcoming a guest into their home. The pilot had popped his hatch and was already halfway out of the craft, reaching back inside for something. He turned, bringing out a canister with a handle and cradling it in one arm as he descended. He reached the ground just as Adam and Alex arrived.

'Captain James?' Adam hoped that their suit radios were set on the same wavelength. The pilot's suit was a much more lightweight, modern design than his own, giving him the uncomfortable feeling that he was dressed in an antique.

The pilot seemed to hesitate. Then he nodded, an action which involved an energetic use of head, shoulders and upper torso; and still he cradled the canister against his body with his arm.

'Do you have any urgent unloads?' Adam lifted his hand to indicate the open hatchway, but the pilot signed no.

Adam let Alex lead the way into the open lock. This seemed to confuse James, who was obviously unclear as to which of his hosts was which. The military set-up of the Saturn Survey placed great emphasis on rank and procedure, and James didn't know whether to take precedence over or give way to the last in the line. Adam rescued him from his uncertainty, inviting him to move on ahead with an expansive gesture.

They filed through the open chamber, passing the dust-smeared buggy with its empty sample hoppers and moving on into the decontamination area. This was a standard feature of the Saturn bases, necessary not because there was any threat from alien organisms but to keep the moon's fine dust out of the station's breathing recycler.

The three figures rocked slightly in the buffeting of the cleaning winds, and Adam reflected with some relief that he was still senior man at Saturn Three. The pilot, as betrayed by his suit flashes, was a probationary handler, probably fresh off the course and making his first solo drop. Technically he was still no more than a Captain and Adam, who had been bumped up to full Major in order to be consigned to the Tethys mausoleum, out-ranked him.

The dying of the bright lights showed that the decontamination was over, and they moved on into the base crewroom. It was a section of the upper level of the main nucleus of the station, a vastly oversized repository for the suits and equipment of a staff of two. One wall was hung with ranks of heavy metal gas bottles, variously coded; the plain, uncoloured bottles were pressurised breathing mixture, whilst the blue and the yellow provided the vapour streams for surface quarrying. Of all the rows, the red-painted bottles were the least scuffed and marked; these were the high pressure burner grenades, rarely needed on cold Tethys.

James took all of this in, and then swung back to look at his hosts. Both had already removed their pressure helmets, and he moved to set the canister down to do likewise. The intention petered out into nothing as he saw Alex.

The girl was more than good-looking – she was actually attractive. This was an age where, thanks to the eugenics boards, looks could be taken for granted or, in extreme cases, bought from a surgical catalogue; but after the innumerable production-line faces of the women at home and on the platform Alex struck him with a freshness that was momentarily arresting. Nobody in space was wearing their hair so long, either; the novelty of this intrigued him further.

'I'd like you to meet my partner,' Adam said, and James realised that he was still helmeted and holding the canister. He set the braincase down and broke the seals around the collar of his suit, lifting the heavy shell clear of his head before setting it down and holding out his hand.

Alex took it, obviously uncertain of the ritual. James

saw that she glanced at the older man for encouragement.

'I guess you don't get a lot of drop-ins on Saturn Three,' James said, as much to break the awkward silence as for any other reason.

'Hardly any,' Alex said with a nervous grin. 'Especially not that have come all the way out from Earth.'

'I've been stationed at the survey platform for a while. It's some time since I made the trip out.'

Adam sensed an unusual enthusiasm from Alex, a kind of rapt attentiveness that always seemed to come over her when Earth was mentioned. She'd never visited the place, and her imagination seemed to enhance its squalor and make it into some unattainable enchanted kingdom.

James broke away and moved towards the ramp which led down to the Central Nucleus of the station, stopping only to lift the braincase canister and take it with him.

'Where are you from?' Adam called after, as he and Alex extracted themselves from their heavy suits.

'My home town's Terminal Five.' The ramp led down into darkness, breaking off into the beginnings of unlit corridors at intervals down its length. He turned, and saw Alex slipping out of the legs of her suit; the thin undersuit clung to her body with static, and James found the sight inexplicably engrossing.

'I know Five,' Adam was saying. 'Whereabouts were you?'

James made an effort to concentrate. She was a girl, that was all – a working equal, available in off-duty hours by mutual agreement. He could approach her later. 'Far side. The East Billions.' Then, when Adam shook his head to show that he didn't know the zone, 'Where were you?'

'I spent a couple of terms in Billion Park. That's some way away from the East zip.'

'They've cleaned it out. It's a dead cell now.'

Adam made a noise of approval. 'I didn't know it, but it's about time. The place was a hole.'

'Yeah. Where isn't?'

Alex watched the conversation attentively, adding to her meagre store of knowledge about Earth.

'Speaking of holes,' James said, looking pointedly around him, 'you know what they say about Saturn Three?'

'We've heard it,' Adam said sharply. It was an old joke, not very pleasant and not very funny, and Adam's affection for Tethys caused him to be offended by its description as the asshole of the solar system.

James didn't seem to be inclined to take off his pressure suit, nor was he going to part with his canister. Adam led the way down the ramp and this time Alex was last in line. James obviously didn't intend to make the same mistake over rank twice.

They came into the general living quarters and James glanced around, unable to conceal a mild amusement.

'Most of what you see is the original station equipment,' Adam explained, conscious of how unfashionable the furnishings must seem to the newcomer and irritated that he should feel it necessary to apologise. 'We don't get many ship-ins from home, and with only the two of us on the base the stuff doesn't get much wear.'

James set the canister down and then let himself drop on to a low divan. He bounced a couple of times, experimentally. 'Takes me back,' he said.

'Don't you have lay-lows on Earth?' Alex asked in surprise.

'Used to, but better than these. These are practically antiques. They don't even mould around you when you sit on them.'

Adam said, 'How is Earth, Captain?'

James' condescending smile froze, and Adam knew

that he'd scored a hit. 'Why do you want to ask a question like that? You get the bulletins, don't you?'

'We acknowledge them, but we don't always make the scan. There's so little that has much bearing on us, Captain.'

There it was again. At the mention of his real rank as opposed to his probationary appointment, James seemed to flinch slightly. Adam decided to remember it; you could never tell when some minor weakness like that might be useful.

Alex brought glasses of amber juice, a vegetable beer with a mild kick that she brewed with one of the experimental yeast cultures from the protein tanks. 'Since you ask about earth,' James said as he accepted a tall glass, 'I can tell you in one word. Hungry.'

'When was she ever anything else?' Adam said. 'The more people you have sitting on the land, the less land you've got to grow them food.'

'What about the seas?' said Alex. 'I thought you were supposed to be farming the seas.'

'Seas are packed with kelp – so much, it rots before you can get it harvested. It's no good and it's not enough. That's why everybody's looking to the Saturn and Jupiter Surveys to come up with a usable protein cake.'

'It's a long way off,' Adam admitted. 'There are so many permutations. About a year ago we got a protein molecule out of the methane – it looked really promising until we started on the acceptability tests. It poisoned half our stock of paramecium.'

'You know Saturn Three's running last on the research scale?'

'I know it,' Adam said, 'but what can we do as long as all the funds and equipment get funnelled into Six on Titan?'

'That isn't exactly the case,' James protested.

'Of course it is. They're not particularly concerned with running a balanced programme. All they want to do is put on a better show than the Jupiter Survey.'

'We've got no contact with the Jupiter Survey.'

'Not on our level. Here on Three we sometimes wonder if we've got any contact with our *own* administration. I'm no biochemist, I'm a spacer. Alex here got basic lab assistant's training on Hyperion before it got closed down, and that's it. We don't even get computer time outside our own facility, so we have to get most of our results on guesswork. Are they really surprised that we're making no progress?'

James spread his hands wide to show that he didn't want to give Adam an argument. 'That's why I'm here.'

'So they send us another robot to keep us happy.'

'Not just another robot,' said James, indicating the canister as if it should mean something to them. 'And anyway, you can hardly complain about being out of contact if you won't even scan the bulletins.'

'No.' Adam made himself smile, tried to force himself to relax. He'd never beaten the drum for Saturn Three before, and wasn't really sure why he was doing it now; the last thing that he could want would be for the base to be run back up to full operational status. Gone would be the calm tranquillity of quiet Tethys, swept away by a cold-faced army of ambitious Service types pouring through its corridors and filling the labs. Gone also would be the open innocence of Alex as she had to learn to adapt to their society, to harden herself to their casual lack of personal feelings.

He was bridling for no other reason than that there was somebody else moving freely around a place that he'd come to regard as his own. Because of these territorial feelings he tended to take offence at James's disdain over the unfashionable fittings of the base, and

24

to seek some crack in James's armour for a retaliation –
hence Adam's pleasure at finding that James was
sensitive about his rank. It was childish. He'd try to put
it out of his mind.

'The message we got said something about a training
period,' he said.

James nodded. 'A few weeks, couple of months at the
most. That's as long as we don't hit problems . . .'

'Are we likely to?'

'It happens.'

Damn right it did. Adam's main hope was that James
would find Saturn Three so unappealing that he would
be spurred on to greater effort in order to leave as soon
as possible. There was only one feature of the base that
James could possibly hope to find comfort in, and Adam
decided to drop a hint on that issue straight away.

'You'll need somewhere to sleep.'

'I suppose I will.'

'You can have Alex's old quarters. She doesn't use
them any more, and it'll save breaking open one of the
old bunkrooms.' Adam paused as James took this in,
noting that his face betrayed no change of expression.
Then Adam turned to Alex. 'As long as that's okay with
you.'

'Sure.' She saw that James's glass was empty, and
added, 'You want another? Or shall I show you to the
quarters now?'

James put the glass to one side. 'Thanks, but there's
something I have to do first.'

'That's okay. You have your own bathroom.'

He smiled at the misunderstanding, but somehow it
didn't spread to his eyes. 'It's not *my* functions I'm
bothered about,' he said, and reached for the cylinder
that he'd kept with him since leaving his spacecraft. 'I
want to get some power into this. I don't want it warm-

ing up until I'm ready for it.'

He didn't offer any further information, so after a moment's pause Adam said, 'Standard lab power be all right for you?'

'Is it variable?'

'Just name your voltage.'

James gave Adam the details of the cylinder's power requirements, and Adam went off to the communications room to reset the links in the racks to give an exact metered flow to the appropriate socket. Alex meanwhile led James, cylinder in hand, down to Saturn Three's research laboratory.

There was a dim UV glow from the hydrophonics tanks at the far end of the chamber, easily the biggest enclosed space in the station. Alex reached for the lights as the tall double-doors closed automatically behind them, and one corner of the lab came into bright illumination. Glancing around as they moved towards a broad white table at the centre of this area James could see the dim shapes of a number of mechanised handling devices and the inert forms of a couple of mobile drones.

'See?' Alex said, noting where his gaze had fallen. 'We've got robots already. Our programme doesn't need them.'

James snorted, unable to disguise his contempt. 'You don't call those *robots*. They're handlers, that's all. Out of date and no damn good. You don't need all that weight and all that mass for the simple jobs they can manage.'

A public address speaker crackled somewhere in the twilight of the lab as James lifted his cylinder and placed it almost reverentially on the white bench.

'I've reset the power level on socket number thirty,' Adam's voice announced, ringing around the lab with a hollow echo. 'That's down the bench on your left.'

James glanced around, surprised. 'Can he see us?' he said to Alex.

'You can see most places from the communications' room. The old security people had cameras everywhere. Seems a shame they wouldn't trust each other.'

'I'm coming down,' Adam's voice went on. 'Be with you in a couple of minutes.'

The speaker crackled and died again as Adam closed the talkback key. James reached for a red wire that was coiled and clipped to his instrument belt, but then seemed to change his mind. His hand hovered over the clip and then undid it slowly, as if he were thinking of something else; he said, without actually looking at Alex, 'Must get lonely here. Just you and him.'

'No,' said Alex, genuinely puzzled. 'Why should it?'

'You could do better,' he told her, unravelling the last couple of loops of the wire and pulling it through his hands to straighten out the kinks. 'I'll talk to you later. When he's not around. In the meantime . . .' he reached into one of the zippered pockets on his suit and brought out a small oblong of plastic, offering it to her. 'You can have these. In case it gets too much.'

'Thanks.' Alex took the object and turned it over. Sealed into numbered transparent bubbles were about half a dozen tiny blue pills. Four of the bubbles had been broken, and the pills removed. 'What are they?'

'Blues. Blue dreamers. Put them away, now.'

She obeyed, stowing them in the breast pocket of her jump suit. James's eyes followed her hands, paying more attention to the backdrop than to the foreground action. Then he jerked his head away as the lab doors slid open and Adam walked in.

'That okay for you?' Adam called out as he approached. Alex turned her head and smiled a greeting.

'Should be okay,' James said. 'I'm just about to try it.' He plugged the shaped connection on the end of the red wire into socket number thirty, recessed into the surface of the bench.

Alex touched the cylinder. The brushed metal had a silky feel, and it was noticably warmer than bloodheat. Must be a radiating surface, she thought.

'No taction contact, please.'

Alex's eyebrows went up. James had snapped out the mechanical phrase as if he were quoting direct from a textbook. 'You mean, don't touch?'

'Correct.' James plugged the other end of the red wire into a receptor at the top of the cylinder, and it began to hum gently.

'Power okay?' Adam asked.

James gave a curt nod. 'It's fine for now.'

'No taction contact,' Alex said musingly.

'That's right.' Obviously James wasn't about to apologise for his sharpness. Perhaps if she'd outranked him . . .

When the readouts on the top of the cylinder had stabilised they moved away from the bench, heading as a group to the door. James indicated that he'd like to call up Survey Base and report his arrival, but Adam said, 'You can't do that.'

James stopped before the doorway, ready for an argument. 'It's not optional. *Sir.*'

Adam was about to speak when Alex interposed with, 'We're in eclipse.'

'Oh. Yes.' James obviously felt foolish, which secretly pleased Adam.

'We don't get any external contact,' Adam explained, 'as long as we're shadow-locked.'

'Of course. How long will it last?'

'Twenty-two days,' supplied Alex.

James was silent for a while as they moved out into the corridor. Adam said, 'You want to see your rooms now?'

'Please. I'm rather tired.'

'I'll show you where they are,' Alex offered before

Adam could say anything.

James followed her down the corridor. Adam couldn't really go along with them, nor was he particularly proud when he found that he wanted to; Alex was an adult, capable of making her own decisions and looking after herself, whilst Adam was too old to be behaving like some jealous adolescent.

Childish, hell, he thought as he watched them disappear around the curve of the station. He wasn't being childish. Captain James was naturally unlikeable.

# FOUR

Alex's old rooms were bare, stripped of all fittings and obviously unused for some considerable time. James stood in the middle of the main chamber, obviously unimpressed; these appointments were spartan indeed compared to those of the platform.

Alex said, 'Dump the sheets in the laundry chute when you want a change. They come back in about four hours.'

James nodded, and continued to look around. There was one of the ubiquitous innocent-looking p.a. speakers angled in one corner, but no sign of a camera. He made no move to suggest that he didn't need any more help, and Alex was uncertain as to whether she should stay or go.

'We run on a standard sixteen-eight day and night,' she said. 'There's about one hour of day to go. Of course, if you're spacelagged or anything like that . . .'

'A little. I've got things to do, first.' Best to be careful in what he said to her, until he could be sure that the Colonel wouldn't be watching. 'My kit's still in the craft.'

'You want me to stay around?'

He turned, and searched for a meaning in her face. There was nothing but an open, honest wish to be of help. 'No,' he said. 'I can manage for myself.'

'Okay . . .' There seemed to be nothing left to say, so Alex backed out of the door and turned to walk back towards the quarters that she shared with Adam. She felt uneasy about leaving James, a stranger, to have a free run of a base that she was used to thinking of as a private home; and yet, she had to remind herself, the base was and always had been a military research establishment, and this hard fact overrode any personal fancy. Besides which, after a while James would be gone, leaving no more significant trace of his presence than another superfluous lab robot. The prospect of this reversion to normal would make James's stay more bearable, and as some compensation he was from Earth. As he settled and relaxed, perhaps he would talk about his home – the sharp manner that he had displayed so far was probably no more than a sympton of his tiredness after the drop.

Adam was stretched out on the bed when she arrived. She hadn't been certain that she would find him here, but it seemed that they shared the feeling that, as long as James was around, this small complex was the only place where they could be assured of privacy.

He flexed his arms over his head as he heard the door slide, giving a groan of luxury as the muscles stiffened by his quarrying work earlier in the shift quivered and tensed before subsiding into relaxation. Tethys's gravity was far too kind to him, as he well knew; although he did the regular isometrics prescribed for all low-gee station personnel he could expect to have a tough time re-adapting to standard density at his age – that is, if he ever had to.

'How's our houseguest settling in?' he asked.

'He seems okay. He says he's got things to do.'

'He probably told you that to stop you quizzing him about Earth.'

'I didn't, Adam, honest.' But there was a playful tone in his voice that suggested he wasn't really serious, so she went on, 'But you couldn't blame me if I did. Not when you never tell me anything about it.'

'What's to tell? Too many people, all shouting for privileges they won't earn. Sitting in their own filth because they won't stoop to clean it up. Always looking for someone to hand them a ready-made answer – and at this moment they're looking at the Surveys. But don't expect them to be grateful if we give it to them.'

'That's just your view,' Alex said, opening the fastenings on her jumpsuit. 'You've always told me I should try to get more than one side of a story before I go making up my mind. That's all I'm trying to do. You seem to forget that I've never really *breathed*.'

'That's not true. You've got all the freedom you can want here, believe me.'

'That's not what I mean. I'm talking about . . . just *breathing*.' There was a hard and unfamiliar shape in one of her pockets, and she reached inside for it. 'And I don't mean machine air, either. Real air, outside, without being shut in.'

Adam seemed to be amused by the idea. 'That's no big deal. Breathing out of doors on Earth is something only disease-freaks do for pleasure.'

'I know. It's just that . . .'

'What do you think of him?' Adam phrased the question as casually as he was able, but it was still false to his own ears. Alex seemed to have trouble coming up with an answer.

'He's . . . funny,' she said at last rather lamely, as if her thoughts had not yet coalesced to give her anything more definite.

'Funny? I must have missed his best lines.'

Adam wondered if he should try to draw her further, but he told himself it wasn't necessary. He wouldn't want to keep her if she didn't want to stay, and if all it took was some jumped-up young space-monkey to shake his confidence – well, he didn't deserve to keep her.

'Adam, what are blues?'

Alex's remark and the half-forgotten name started

pulling his mind into reluctant focus. He lifted himself on one elbow; she was sitting on the end of the bed, half out of her jumpsuit and holding up a slim oblong of a type that he had not seen for some years; a six-month supply of blue dreamers, the spacer's analgesic for fear and loneliness. Take one a week for a hallucinatory trip of such pleasurable credibility that the discomfort of temporal reality paled and became bearable – as long as you had another trip to look forward to. To Adam they were a crutch for an inadequate mind.

'Where did you get those?' he said, sitting up and reaching for the pills. Alex handed them over.

'He gave them to me.'

'He had no business. These things are dangerous.' There were four missing, but obviously Alex hadn't taken any – she'd have been hovering several inches off the ground. It was hard enough for Adam to face that he might lose Alex in open competition with the society beyond Tethys; all he had to offer was himself, and he could hardly bear to think that his trade goods of modest worth might be further devalued in a drug-clouded judgement.

Alex couldn't understand his anger. They were a few blue tablets, that was all. 'What do they do?' she asked, bewildered.

'If they send someone out alone, they give him some to keep him from going over the top.' There was a further insult in that James obviously thought Alex might need them.

'Did you ever use them?'

'Me?'

'You told me you were on your own sometimes when you were on the Venus slingshot. Didn't you have them then?'

'No.' Then he admitted, 'But I had them once.'

'Really? When?'

'A long time ago and a long way away.' He couldn't bring himself to tell her that, once, blue dreamers had been the only way that he could bear to stay on her precious Earth, and that even these had, in the end, been inadequate.

'What was it like?'

He shrugged, trying to play it down. 'Interesting.'

'Why don't we try it? Together, I mean.'

'Maybe.'

'Please?'

He had to remember that she had been starved of the unusual, whilst he on the other hand had been more than sated by it. 'After James has gone,' he promised, secretly hoping that she would forget. 'But you mustn't be disappointed.'

'Disappointed? Why?'

'They're not a patch on taction contact.'

They both laughed. James was an odd outsider and would stay that way. 'I'll try to make sure he doesn't stay any longer than necessary,' Adam said, 'but remember he'll have a report to make. Do your best to make him feel at home, won't you?'

'Not my *best*,' Alex said with exaggerated coyness, and leaned across the bed to place a light kiss on Adam's forehead. Then she rolled over to kick off the legs of her jumpsuit before sliding under the sheets.

There was a howling, a thin strained sound from somewhere down the corridor. Adam sighed and closed his eyes in irritation – the damn dog had got herself shut in the lab again.

Sally was the most complex organism they had for the testing of any proteins that their experimentation produced. So far they'd never tested on anything higher than the most simple one-celled animals, but they had a range of frozen embryos that they could revive and grow to test the metabolic acceptability of any promising-looking molecules. If it didn't kill the amoebae, try it on the fish; and then from the fish to the gecko, and then the frog, the rat and finally the dog. If an experiment reached the dog stage it was big news, and the Survey would start pulling primates from routine maintenance tasks and shipping them down for further tests.

Strictly speaking, Sally should have remained as an embryo in stasis until she was needed, but Adam found dogs to be inoffensive, occasionally appealing animals, and he suspected that Alex might feel the same way. He had broken out the embryo block and hooked it into an amniotic tank without telling Alex, and then presented her with the puppy as a surprise.

Now Sally was exhibiting her happy knack of demanding attention just when they were least inclined to give it.

'I'll go,' Alex said, sliding off the bed.

'Put something on,' Adam warned her. 'Remember we don't have the place to ourselves right now.'

She took a light robe from her locker and pulled it around herself, knotting the waist cord as she stepped out into the corridor. The whining came from the direction of the lab, a place where Sally often wandered in with one of them to curl up in a quiet corner as they worked; when she woke up alone, her small body was insufficient to trigger the door-opening sensors.

Halfway around, the corridor lights died. At least, that was Alex's momentary impression as the day effect faded without warning to the nightsight setting, but after she'd paused for a moment as her eyes readjusted she was able to go on.

The dog was definitely trapped in the laboratory, as the sounds of canine anguish became closer and more easily localised. Alex was puzzled; the last time she'd

35

seen Sally had been while Adam was out in the buggy, and then the dog had been stretched out on top of the insulated cover of the heat-exchanger in the upper Nucleus. She hadn't followed any of them into the lab later, so how did she come to be there?

The lab doors whisked open as Alex approached, and a dim slice of light from the corridor speared in and startled the whimpering animal that had been pawing at the unyielding exit. Alex made meaningless placatory noises as she gathered the small mongrel into her arms and then turned to go.

James's mysterious canister still hummed on the bench that had been allotted to him. Alex hesitated for a moment, the dog now quietened by getting what it felt to be its just measure of attention, and then moved across the lab for a closer look. The doors hissed shut as she moved out of sensor range.

The UV glow of the hydroponics tanks was enough for Alex's night-tuned eyes to make out the detail of the cylinder. Shifting Sally's weight mainly on to her left arm she reached out with her free hand and touched the silky facing of the metal.

The cylinder reacted immediately. Its top eased out an inch or so and began a silent rotation through one hundred and eighty degrees. As the hollow interior of the canister became exposed a soft light formed a haze over the opening, and Alex stood on tiptoe to look inside.

The hand fell heavily on her shoulder. 'No taction contact,' James barked.

Alex shrieked and Sally joined in, wriggling free and dropping to the floor as Alex jerked back from James's unexpected touch. With a scrabbling of claws on the smooth composition surface the dog was away and out of sight in the deep shadows at the far side of the lab.

James reached across and touched something on the

36

canister lid, causing it to slide slowly back into place. 'I said not to touch it,' he told Alex. 'I meant it.'

Alex wanted to come back with an angry rebuke, but she knew she was in the wrong. Instead she turned away from James and moved across the lab, calling to the dog.

Obviously Sally had seen James as he had passed through the upper nucleus after bringing in his kit from the spacecraft. The inquisitive animal had followed him down to the lab and come through the open doors behind him. But then, it seemed, he had ignored the dog's plaintive whining to get out; and what disturbed Alex even more was that he had clearly waited in the shadows after she herself had come in, watching her without making his presence known.

Sally had wormed her way into the narrow gap between two of the tanks, and Alex called her name to coax her out.

'The dog has a *name*?' James seemed to find this remarkable. So remarkable in fact, that he came over for a closer look, and Alex wanted to back away from his approaching silhouette. But she stood her ground.

'Of course she has a name,' Alex said. She rather wished that she'd switched on the lab's full lighting, but the control was over by the door. 'Didn't you ever have a dog?'

'A few times.' Without a view of James's face, Alex was struck by the peculiar lack of feeling in his voice. 'First time I've ever heard of one having a name, though.'

'There's nothing unusual in it.'

'Obviously we've been looking at different menus.'

Was he being honest, or was he baiting her? It was impossible to tell.

'Sally's not something on a menu. She's a pet.' Encouraged by the mention of her name, the dog came snuffling out of her hideaway and, with a wary sideways glance at the dark form of the man who had sent her there, allowed herself to be lifted for the second time.

'Where I come from, a dog's a food animal. Sentiment's a luxury we don't allow ourselves.' The shadow turned briefly into profile, that hunted, predator-shy action that Alex had noted earlier when James had learned of the cameras around the station. The darkness of the lab seemed to satisfy his fear of being observed, and he turned back to Alex. She held the dog up before her, a soft and inadequate shield.

'I guess we should be going to bed,' Alex said nervously.

James spoke softly. 'Ready when you are.'

It was a moment before Alex realised what he meant. James seemed to sense her indignation, and added, 'I was only looking for hospitality. I appreciate your body and I'd like to use it.'

'No,' Alex said firmly. 'I'm with the Major. I *like* to be with the Major.'

'For his personal use only. That's unsocial on Earth, you know? You could even be punished for it.'

'Maybe. But that's how we do things on Saturn Three.' She pushed past him, and he made no move to stop her.

Adam was in the corridor outside their quarters when she got back, a robe like her own thrown loosely about him.

'You seemed to be a while,' he said.

'He was in there.'

They walked the last few yards together. 'I know,' Adam said. 'I took a look.'

'How?'

'I used the monitor in the room and switched the cameras over to infra-red. He gave you quite a scare, didn't he?'

'It was my own fault. Taction contact.'

38

'What? Your mistake or his request? As soon as we're out of eclipse and he's through with his mission, out he goes. If you get any problems, don't forget that I out-rank him.'

'You may,' Alex said, 'but I don't.'

They came to the door of their shared quarters. 'Any problems,' Adam told her, 'and you just report them in to the Major.'

'Major,' Alex said solemnly. 'I have a problem.'

'Well?'

'I love you.'

Adam placed his hand over the biocapacitance sensor, and the door hissed open. 'Come into my quarters,' he said, 'and I'll ease your problem.'

# FIVE

As usual, Adam second-guessed the station's automatic timer and was out of bed before the corridors and work areas switched over to daylight levels. This was usually a matter of no importance, as the sleeping quarters lighting systems were isolated from those of the rest of the base; but as he emerged from the bathroom towelling his hair after a refreshing hot shower he noticed that the video monitor across from the bed still carried the image of the lab from the 'night' before. It was the Station Commander's spy-eye, and Adam had never had any reason to use it when only he and Alex were about the base. He'd forgotten to switch it off, and as the lab warmed with the daytime heat rise the monitor faithfully brightened in its infra-red reproduction.

Behind him, Alex slid out of bed and moved into the bathroom. Adam reached to kill the image and then had second thoughts, switching first from the infra-red to normal spectrum viewing, and then dialling slowly through the cameras at various sites around the base.

James was nowhere to be seen – at least, not in the public areas that the cameras covered. Adam mechanically punched up corridor followed by corridor followed by general view of the Central Nucleus . . .

He stopped, and went back to the camera in the outer hangar. The scene was peaceful enough, but something seemed wrong; looking more closely, Adam could see that the buggy was missing from its usual parking place. His hand went straight to the end of the rank of buttons to give him an outside view of the station.

Alex had emerged from the bathroom and now came to stand behind his shoulder, watching the image as it frame-rolled and then steadied.

James had driven the buggy right up to the ladder on the spiderleg of his spacecraft. Detail was good and clear, being picked out in crisp silhouette against Saturn's high-level reflection. At one time, when man's knowledge of planet-forming processes was, to say the least, sketchy, it had been believed that the brilliance of Saturn was partly due to heat that was internally generated. Fortunately for the scholars who offered this theory they never had to walk on the planet's surface, offering as it did a temperature of two-ninety below.

From the waist up James was swallowed by his spacecraft, leaning in through the open hatchway. Adam operated a rocket switch to tighten the field of view, and the camera obligingly began to collapse the perspective of the picture.

'Looks like he's not travelling light,' Adam commented as a load consisting of three bulky metal crates on the platform of the buggy slid past the field of view. James was wrestling with the mass of a fourth crate, managing it with care although its weight under Tethys's light pull was no real problem.

'Perhaps he's going to build his own place,' Alex said.

Adam was all for the idea. 'Maybe we should help him.'

'I don't think so. He's here to help us, isn't he?'

So they had breakfast, and only then went to see what James was doing. He had transferred all four of the cases through the airlock and the decontamination chamber and then carried them, one by one, down the ramp and into the lab. Although their weight under the regime of Tethys's gravity was considerably reduced the work had obviously cost James some effort; when Alex and Adam came upon him they noticed an audible drone from the units on his pressure suit as they struggled to draw off his excess body heat.

'That's quite a lot of equipment,' Adam commented as James was unsealing the side-fastenings on his suit. James nodded absently, the complaints of his suit units dying as he shrugged out of the gloved sleeves and let the garment fall to the floor. He stepped out of it and bundled it on to an adjacent bench, his interest more on the cases before him. Adam and Alex exchanged a glance. What kind of space-monkey was it that neglected basic suit safety care? And a so-called *handler*, no less?

James's undersuit was damp with effort, his hair pushed into moist spikes by a careless rub of the sleeve across his forehead. He walked around the cases, trying to decide which to open first.

Adam said, 'How long do you think this will take?'

'I don't know. Until I'm done.'

With this enigmatic estimate James lifted the crates in order on to the bench. They filled it from one end to the other, and he went along the row with a metal punch. A thin covering of foil in the centre of each peeled back to reveal a strong handle, and as the handles were turned each case gave an audible sigh as the pressure within equalised to that of the base.

James returned to the first of the cases and lifted its side away. Alex moved around behind him to take a look at the contents. The crash foam wadding was already melting and running as contact with air destroyed it, but the maze of interlocked parts meant little to her.

'Doesn't really look much like a robot,' she said.

'It wouldn't,' James replied, reaching into the case and taking a careful hold of one of the components. 'This kind of organism doesn't bear any kind of relation to the simple work-and-feedback devices you'll have experience of. This is one of the first of the Demigod series.'

Adam thought it a rather pretentious title for a kit that came through the mail, but he was familiar with the way in which the Survey engineers liked to dramatise their achievements. He'd once been shipped a *Respiration Sentinel* which was suppose to be plumbed into his pressure suit airline and would perform the invaluable task of telling him whether or not he was breathing.

The part that James had withdrawn from the first case was undoubtedly a hand. Adam could appreciate that it was an element in a far more complex mechanism than any of their general-duty lab robots, for whilst their manipulating claws required three separate joints and servo motors to approximate the range of movement of a real hand the Demigod seemed to contain all the necessary flexibility in a single, aesthetically attractive unit.

James turned the hand over, and the fingers fell open in a response as relaxed and natural as that of a fresh corpse.

It took several hours for all the parts to be removed from their cases and laid carefully on the bench. Most of them were prewired and preconstructed module units, but even so it was impossible to look at them and get any impression of what the final assembly might be like. Adam soon got bored and said loudly that he had work to do; Alex seemed happy to stay and watch, and so Adam was forced to act alone on his announcement. Once outside the lab he looked around, wondering how he should now occupy himself. He'd wander up to the main social area, perhaps run a show tape, play some muzak. Although he wouldn't admit it to himself, he was tempted to go up to the communications room and tune in to the lab camera. What a ridiculous idea. No reason for it at all.

Alex had the feeling that James was working self-consciously. She wondered whether to ask if her presence disturbed him, but that didn't seem to be the reason at all; it was almost as if he were aware of being watched by someone else altogether, someone from whom he had something to fear. Could it be Adam? That was silly. Adam was no ogre.

Nevertheless, James didn't seem inclined to make any conversation. He only spoke in reply to a direct question from her, and even then he appeared to be unwilling to meet her eye. His glance roved over the laid-out innards of the potential mechanical entity as he answered, an insecure, repetitive action that betrayed far more about his state of mind than his normally inexpressive speech.

'Will you assemble all of this yourself?'

'Not entirely.'

'How, then?'

'I'll do the main module hookups. I can use your lab robots to do the rest.'

'But they won't be programmed for that kind of assembly.'

'They don't need to be. The Demigod contains all the programming they'll need. They'll be under the Demigod's direct control.'

And so it went on. When Adam eventually wandered back into the lab the components were all laid out and the cases had been cleared away. All attention was focused on the cylinder that James had cherished with such care since his arrival.

Adam moved around the lab to get a better view. The overhead lights had been dimmed, and the lid of the canister had rotated away so that its internal lighting was spilling out. Alex flashed him a quick smile of greeting, too absorbed in the revelation of this small

44

mystery to do more; James glanced up briefly but made no sign of recognition.

Cold gases were boiling off, but the light from within the cylinder was warm. As soon as it was safe to do so James reached over and began to withdraw a transparent inner block. After he had raised it a few inches he took his hand away and it continued to ease upward under its own power, throwing out more light as it came.

The object within the block was unimpressive, visually a disappointment were it not for the fact that its function was unmistakable. Two litres of softy grey tissue the density of water, suspended in fluid and held by a network of filaments carefully placed to put no strain on any one part of the organ. It was shaped into an oval, free of the moulding pressures of development within a skull and with a surface that was evenly crimped like the sea's forlorn message on a deserted beach.

'Is it human?' said Alex.

'It was, once,' said James.

It was as yet unborn, free of intellect and sensation; basic programming was contained elsewhere in the Demigod's pseudo-nervous system, ready for use as soon as the tissue was brought into full awareness.

'How long will it take to programme?' Adam asked.

'Couple of days to fix up the body. Then, once it's grasped the idea of what it's supposed to be doing . . . about three, four weeks.'

Adam was impressed in spite of himself. 'As quickly as that?'

'I told you when I arrived how long I'd be staying.'

'Yes, but . . .' The brain tissue seemed curiously naked and powerless in the soft light of the heating element that was bringing it up to the threshold of a twilight form of life. 'Three weeks . . . it takes a human baby about twenty years to become a basic space-monkey.

How are you going to manage the same job in three weeks?'

'I know what I'm doing. As soon as I get his head together he'll take over your programme for you. All he'll need is a regular twelve hour charge. May as well face it – one of you's going to be obsolete.'

# SIX

As the realisation sank in it was a time for closeness, for consolation, for intelligent reassurance. But they sat on opposite sides of the bed and stared at different walls.

'It needn't be a disaster,' Alex said after a while. Her voice struck her as sounding odd, too crisp in the depressive silence. 'I don't see why we shouldn't get another mission. The two of us in the same place. Is that so unlikely?'

'I don't know,' said Adam.

There was another pause as Alex tried to think of arguments to justify the proposal. 'We've got to find a way to stay together,' she said lamely after an interval.

'You're too young.'

'Too young for what?'

'For me, among other things.'

'You never minded it before.'

'I don't *mind* it now. But you can't waste yourself in a place like this forever. Perhaps it's just me that's too old.'

'Not for me.'

'Maybe not, but it's the Survey's word that counts when it comes to allocating missions.'

Alex turned, angry at Adam's implied dismissal of his own abilities. 'You're as good as any spacer they've got. Every time you test you still come out A-one, Tethys gravity or no Tethys gravity.'

'Okay, so to you I'm *ubermensch*. To them I'm still old.'

'But . . .'

'They don't *go* by the grading. When you reach your abort time they pull you out, wrap you up and put you carefully on one side. They don't want decrepit spacers fouling up on the job. I thought that here they might forget about me – they seem to think so little about Saturn Three most of the time . . .'

'. . . but old Mother Earth never seems to forget.'

'No.' Adam's mind began to wander, seeking refuge in alternate and momentary realities. 'We could send him for a buggy ride. Rig the pumps to overpower the drive. He'd bump over the ridge and hit escape velocity without realising it. We could send his boxes of scrap along with him.' He paused, and thought a little more. 'Then – when we get out of eclipse – we could enter a non-arrival on him.'

'You wouldn't do that.'

Adam considered it. 'It happens all the time, all over the solar system. Procedures get skipped, precautions get ignored. A pile goes into meltdown and a moon blows. A hatch pops and there's another ruptured space-monkey in orbit.'

Alex couldn't raise enthusiasm for such macabre and pointless speculation, and she knew Adam far too well to think that he might be serious. 'That's horrible,' she said tonelessly.

'It's not really horrible. It's very practical when you consider it.' He sighed, watching the dream dissipate and the unpleasantness of the moment return. 'It's also murder, and I'm not really update enough for that kind of jag. If I was like James, I might be serious. Maybe it would be better if I *was* like James.'

'I'm glad you're not,' said Alex.

Over the next few days James occupied himself with the assembly of the Demigod, and Adam wasn't too worried about what he did as long as it kept him away from James. This left Alex somewhere in the middle; Adam was around but strangely unavailable, and James had become too self-absorbed to be drawn into conversation about his Earth home. He appeared not to leave the lab at all, a passing glance at the communications room monitors showing that he worked on as Adam and Alex went to bed at the end of that day period and returned to the occupation – if, indeed, he had ever left it for a few hours of stolen sleep – well before they awoke the next morning.

Alex had some work to do but it was nothing urgent, certainly nothing that couldn't wait until James had finished his intensive assembly. Occasionally she'd take him food or a glass of amber juice. He'd thank her automatically, take a bite or a couple of sips, and then push the nourishment aside saying that he'd return to it later.

Neither of them made any reference to that first night in the unlit lab. In the moments when her mind sought refuge from the contemplation of the bleak prospect of an unwanted separation Alex would reflect on the aggressive formality of James's approach to her. The more she considered it, the more certain she was that it had really been a mistake, a misunderstanding caused by a wide difference in social background. *I appreciate your body and I'd like to use it.* He couldn't know that he would frighten and offend her, accustomed as she was to the fierce sexual possessiveness of the frontier stations; perhaps he was now as embarrassed as she had been, and this accounted to some extent for his withdrawal into his work.

As this theory filled out and took shape Alex began to feel almost guilty. She had no reason to want to ingratiate herself with James, but nor did she want to be unfair to him; and in her social naïvety, untoughened as she was by the abrasion of the unkind and the uncouth, she was unable to dismiss from her mind the possibility that, in his silence, he might be thinking ill of her.

Adam had found his own retreat, digging out long-neglected station safety procedures and following through the checks with meticulous care. He told Alex that he'd been forgetful, and that the inspection was long overdue. He set about it with the diligent care of a clear-headed invalid ordering his worldly affairs.

When Alex next wandered into the lab the work seemed to have progressed little. Small unidentifiable units had become larger unidentifiable units, but they were not yet positioned in the body shell. Biological chauvinism dictated that it was impossible to think of the Demigod as a functional entity before it had a degree of corporeal integrity.

Perhaps that chauvinism wasn't entirely groundless. The robot would, after all, incorporate cultured brain tissue; grown in a laboratory tank, of course, but still of a sufficiently human origin to promise a difficult blurring of the distinction between man and machine. Other parts under construction suggested that the biological overlap might not be limited to the brain alone; there was a clear jar filled with colour-coded soft, moist tubing, and carboys of thick liquid which, in blue and orange, seemed like a veinous and arterial parody.

James had two of the lab's stumpy drone robots working for him, and he was also making use of some of the remote handling devices. The bench was a maze of activity, and even the massive overhead crane had been brought in at one stage; now discarded, it had been rolled back near the lab doors and Alex had to step around it as she entered.

James was standing back, watching the Demigod take shape. Most of his work was now done in the basic assembly of the nervous system; now the Demigod, diffuse as it was, had taken over its own creation.

He had heard the zip of the lab doors, and he looked up as Alex came around the crane.

'I was wondering . . .' she said hesitantly, wary of another misinterpretation, 'I was wondering if you needed anything.'

'Not really. You have work of your own.'

'I don't have much to do unless Adam brings back a new set of surface samples on the buggy. Then I have to melt them down and measure off the contaminations before we introduce the different bacteria. They do the rest.'

James's face betrayed the slightest flicker of interest. 'The Major? Is he out in the Rover now?'

'No. He's checking the outer plate seals.'

'You mean he's outside?'

'That's not necessary. The indicators are all around the inner shell. Takes a while to get around them, though.'

James nodded, and was quiet was quiet for a moment. The articulated claws of the lab robots darted in and out with speed and precision.

'I was right, wasn't I,' he said with an abrupt switch of subject, 'that you're space-born?'

'Yes, I am. I've never seen Earth.'

'It puzzled me. Spaceborn aren't supposed to have names. And yet he calls you Alex.'

She felt a knot of tension suddenly pull tight within her in response to his probing. 'It's the name he gave me.'

'And only he can use it, right?'

'That's right.'

Still with his eyes on the Demigod, he shook his head with a half sad, half superior smile. 'You know, you'll have to forget that kind of sentiment when you get to Earth.'

'Who says I'm going there?'

'One of you is. And at his age, he'll never survive more than a year back at full gee.'

'Adam's not old . . .'

'He's old enough. You get used to this kind of life and the heart can't take the strain. No point shipping him all the way back when he can still be of some use here. They'll leave him to help Hector.'

'Who?'

James indicated the activity before them. 'Eldest son of Priam, defender of Troy.' It meant nothing to her. He went on, 'His brother Paris loved Helen and took her away from her husband. When the husband came to get her back, Hector was there to stand by his brother.'

'Who won?' said Alex.

James seemed to become disenchanted with the analogy. 'It doesn't matter. What you've got to think about is that when the Demigod takes over you'll probably be shipped out of here. You're going to have to get used to Earth ways pretty fast.'

'I'm not sure I like the sound of Earth ways.'

'That won't matter a damn. No names for the Spaceborn, that's the law. And no personal possession of people, that's the law too.'

'Let's stay impersonal, shall we, *Captain*?'

James was plainly stung by the trick she had picked up from Adam, but he controlled his annoyance. He changed his approach, lowering his voice and looking directly at her. She found it discomforting.

'I know why you won't show me hospitality,' he said.

'The station's yours,' Alex replied tightly. 'Anything you're entitled to, you can have.'

'I'm talking about *you*. I think you're afraid of the Major.'

'I'm not afraid of anybody.'

52

'You're scared he'll be jealous. All right, so he gets jealous. What does it matter? Couple of months and you'll be moving out. You want to dump him before that, you can move in with me.'

'I've got no intention of moving in with you.'

'Think again and you'll see it's the only way.' He stabbed a finger up towards the ceiling, in the general direction of where he thought the Survey platform might be. 'It's a completely different world out there, and, believe me, you won't last a week. Right now I'm the only useful friend you've got.'

'I don't need any help from you.'

'Come on, Alex. I've seen the way your eyes light up every time Earth gets mentioned. You've always wanted to see it and you won't be happy until you do – all Spaceborn are like that, it's natural. What you've got here – you and him – that's all that's holding you back, don't you see?'

'You can't understand. And don't call me Alex.'

His eyes narrowed, and he leaned towards her. 'I'm no loser,' he said. 'Remember that. And don't try to tell me you don't want to see Earth.'

'Some day,' she admitted, 'maybe. But we do things differently here on Tethys. Please remember *that*, Captain.'

Adam flicked the switch to kill the picture on the bedroom monitor. The silent image of the lab faded and he sat quietly for a few moments, his eyes on the blank screen and his mind far away. Then he moved slowly to the bathroom to shower away the sweat and grease of his crawl along the station's inner shell.

# SEVEN

Still A-one. For some reason Adam seemed to be throwing himself into his isos with renewed enthusiasm since James's arrival. Even he wasn't entirely sure whether he was impelled by an uneasy sense of competition from the younger man, or whether it was the prospective dangers of a return to a more demanding environment that led him to set muscle against muscle in non-productive strain.

Alex had seen the spacers' ritual before, and even had a similar exercise sequence herself; as far as man might spread and settle, Earth was always home and the planet's physical conditions dictated the health and strength of the organism. Laxity in low-gee gave eventual muscular and circulatory problems along with a gradual loss of bone calcium; physical jerks and metered mineral intake, directed by a feedback of regular checkups, were the spacers' survival programme.

She sat on a low beam in Saturn Three's small but fully-equipped gymnasium, and watched as Adam completed the last of his routines. He'd acknowledged her as she'd entered, but his efforts were too strenuous to allow him to speak; and as he braced himself against the wall and tried to drag tempered steel bars out of their concrete mounts she thought about James's estimate of the Major's prospects on Earth.

Adam was in better shape than many men half his age. His pulse rate invariably rose in a smooth curve throughout the routine, flattening out well within acceptable limits, and the cardiogram showed a steady and well-tempered beat. James himself hadn't set foot in the gym since his arrival although, as with all the station's facilities, it was freely available to him.

All the station's facilities except one, Alex reminded herself grimly. And perhaps he was prepared to lie and exaggerate to gain access to that.

'What's it like,' she asked as Adam completed the bar-pull and moved across to the scales, 'being under full gee?'

'It's not *like* anything. It's just something you get used to. You'll find out when you get to Earth.'

'But I'm not going.'

'You've always wanted to.'

'And you've always told me I'll be disappointed. Who wants to go all that way just to be disappointed?'

He read off the numbers on the digital display, and then touched the key which would automatically correct them to Earth-normal. 'I'm old and jaded. You shouldn't take my word for anything.'

'Whose word should I take? Not James's, I'm sure.'

'Just because he's unlikeable, it doesn't mean everything he says should be dismissed. What's he been telling you?'

'Nothing much. But if what he says about the Demi-god is true . . .'

Adam smiled. 'I'll believe it when I see it,' he said, but there was a hollowness to his words that he couldn't completely conceal.

Alex pressed the point. 'But if it happens. If they decide to cut the staff on Saturn Three to one . . .'

'. . . then I'll have to stay and you'll have to go – you don't have the rank to stay on as nominal commander.'

'But that means they'll be splitting us up. That's not what you want, is it?'

'Maybe it's for the best,' he said, and hoped it sounded convincing. It should – it was costing him enough effort and determination. 'You want to see Earth, and I'd guess that he's asked you to go with him. Is that right?'

'He's said I won't have any choice. I don't believe him.'

'Whether you get the choice or not, you're wasting yourself here. Saturn Three's just a backwater in the System – it's all right for an ageing spacer like me, but you've hardly started out. You can't let your whole life go rambling by in a dusty corner like this.' He tried to keep his voice light, his manner casual as the undercurrent of agony grew. One day, perhaps, he would be able to extract some minor satisfaction from his act of sacrifice, but such a day seemed impossibly far away.

Alex was bewildered. 'You don't want us to stay together?'

'It's not what *I* want. That doesn't count. I'm thinking of you.'

'Well, I don't want to leave.'

'Of course you do. You've always wanted to see Earth.'

'But you've always said that I'd hate it.'

'Maybe I was only being selfish, trying to slap you down and keep you here. Getting all your ideas second-hand is no way to live. And that's all you'll do if you keep on getting your opinions from me – you may hate Earth, you may love it. But at least find out for yourself.'

'With *him*? No thanks.'

Her rejection of James in such positive terms gave Adam strength to continue. 'But all that apart. You still want to go, don't you?'

Her bewildered indignation deflated a little. 'Of course,' she admitted. 'I always have. Even if I hate every minute of it, something inside draws me back there. I can't describe it to you, Adam – you're not

Spaceborn, you can't know how insecure it makes you feel to be out on the fringes and never really have a sense of belonging. But I don't want it if it's on his terms – and I don't want it if it's without you.'

Adam shrugged, a little gesture of futility. As much as his own inner defences might crumble, he could fall back upon an immovable buttress of logic. 'It won't really be our choice. Looks like James and his Demigod are going to make the decision for us.'

They moved away from the scales and approached the records terminal, a typewriter input on a wheeled dolly in the corner of the gym.

'It doesn't necessarily follow,' Alex said as they walked.

'I'm afraid it does.' Adam tapped in his personal code and began to transfer across the brief details of the exercise session for comparison and monitoring purposes. 'The survey's run by a machine just like this one. It doesn't laugh, it doesn't cry, it doesn't care – apart from caring for the things it's been programmed to pay attention to. Like efficiency and economy and damn-all else.'

'You said you're close to abort time. Ready to be pulled out and put one one side, and we already know that there's no chance of *me* being left here alone. What's wrong with us both going together?'

'They've got to decide to pull me first.'

'They will. You said they don't want decrepit spacers messing things up.'

His eyebrows lifted. 'Well, thanks!'

'Survey doesn't know what kind of shape you're in. All it will have to go on when it checks will be the records in the base computer.'

'Which in my case are a consistent A-one, apart from the time I picked up some bug from one of the lab cultures. They're not going to pull me until the very last moment as long as I've got a record like that.'

'Right. So this morning I jinxed the records for you.'

His hand paused in mid air over the terminal keys. 'You did what?'

'I've got the basic training, it was easy. I went back as far as the time you were ill and down-graded all the results consistently. Survey says that Saturn Three's behind schedule. We know it's because we don't get back-up, but the Survey computer only knows what it's told; it won't take account of the way that everybody gives priority to Six. When it sees your record it will think that it's the reason for the trouble, and you'll be pulled. They'll replace you, and we can go to Earth together.'

Adam didn't know what to say. His arguments, his sacrifice, all his efforts at persuasion seemed to be draining away inside. Alex misunderstood his momentary silence, and said hurriedly, 'I kept a tape of all the original data. If it isn't what you want, I can put the records back the way they were and nobody will ever know.'

He shook his head. He could no longer press an issue for which he felt no conviction against such determined resistance. 'If you want me,' he said simply, 'I'll come.'

'To Earth?'

'If it makes you happy.'

'I'm sure I'll hate it, but I need to see it some day. And I'd rather we hated it together.'

Alex cancelled the input on the terminal and retyped Adam's results, reducing the efficiency levels of each to a slight degree. Adam watched her at work and began to laugh, suppressing it at first but then laughing out loud. This devious, capable side of her nature was one that he had never seen before; perhaps he should thank James for helping to bring it out. Alex started to giggle, and Adam was reassured; his greatest worry had always been that contact with the harsher forces that prevailed outside the comfortable world of the station would be Alex's destruction. Now it seemed that the opposite was true, and he could only marvel at the inadequacy of his own judgement.

They were still laughing when Alex finished the input and signed off the terminal. He put his arm around her shoulder, her slight form fitting in against his side as if by design as they moved towards the gym doors.

'Hold me up, I'm a decrepit old spacer,' he pleaded in a quavering voice, and she raised an admonitory finger for a half-serious reproach.

The gym doors shot apart abruptly and half a ton of glittering metal stumbled into the chamber, barely under control and swaying dangerously. Adam jumped back and pulled Alex with him as the robot took another faltering step and threatened to overbalance on to them, and when Alex squealed it tried to turn in the doorway, obviously confused.

James was in the corridor, blocked from entering by the intervening bulk. 'Don't make noise,' he was shouting, 'he has to be able to hear me!'

The robot took another stride but stopped half-way, as if it were uncertain of its ability to stay upright if it completed the move. This gave James sufficient room to squeeze through into the gym.

'Stand, Hector,' he said. 'Stand!'

Hector hesitated, and then carefully drew his trailing foot level and shuffled into a reasonably stable stance, servos whining and whirring to make the necessary minute adjustments in his posture. The Demigod was a full head taller than either Adam or James, and his outward design reflected his name. His bodyshell was like classical armour, pressed and sculpted into a semblance of muscle and sinew with necessary compromises for the placing of sockets and displays. Legs and torso were almost human in their moulding, narrow hips and waist rising in a series of overlapping gold plates to massive shoulders and chest, but the arms and the sensory apparatus were of a more utilitarian design. There was no head, as such; between the shoulders was a swivelling turret on which was mounted a triple-jointed anglepoise mechanism carrying a single sensory eye.

'You frightened him,' James said reproachfully.

## EIGHT

Hector lumbered along to the lab, with James calling out instructions for every turn or change of pace. The Demigod seemed to have no formed intellect of its own, only an imperfectly developed motor system which responded to direct command and continued in the response until it was told to stop. Every move suggested uncertainty and a degree of misjudgement that was sometimes hastily corrected, more often not. Twice the Demigod lurched into the curving wall of the corridor, unable to modify its linear advance without advice.

Nevertheless, it heard and understood, and was able to take the correct action once that action had been identified to it. This was considerably in advance of the lab robots, which needed a painstakingly set-up programme to break down every routine into the simplest stages, and which could never divert from that programme although, once remembered, they could repeat it indefinitely. The Demigod could learn by instruction or by observation, and it had an added – although admittedly sub-human – capacity to synthesise that learning into basic forms of judgement and understanding.

'The real programming hasn't even begun yet,' James insisted as Hector squared up to the lab doors and prepared to march straight through, whether they opened or not. James quickly put his hand within range of the biocapacitance sensor, and the doors flew apart. This would be a problem; some system would have to be devised whereby Hector would be able to open doors for himself. 'All I was aiming at,' James went on as they followed the Demigod through into the lab, 'was a demonstration of the basic nerve responses.'

'Whose nerves?' Adam demanded. 'His, or ours?'

'One of you is going to have to live with him. It's as well you get some idea of what he can or can't do right from the start. Once he's learned some measure of self-control . . .'

'Until he does, I want him kept away from all the living and recreation areas. Is that understood?'

'You're not being fair,' James protested. 'The brain-case was powered less than an hour ago. You can't take what you've seen as a conclusive demonstration of his abilities.'

'Until I decide better, that's exactly what I'm going to do. Without control he's a potential danger and I want him kept well away from Alex.' Adam turned to the girl. She was standing some way back from the Demigod, eyeing the machine warily. 'We don't know the instruction vocabulary. I think we'd best keep Hector in here until we know he can be trusted outside.' Then, back to James, 'Neither of us will come into the lab unless you're here, and even then we'll probably come together.'

'All this isn't necessary. It won't take me more than a few hours to set up a basic intellect. After that he'll be as safe as anything.'

'Safe for you, perhaps.'

'Safe for anybody.' James turned to Alex. There was a note of desperation in his voice, a need for self-justification. 'Try him. Give him a simple instruction.'

Alex glanced at Adam, and Adam nodded. She looked around the lab for inspiration, and then said, 'Hector . . . would you please give that micrometer to the Major?'

The Demigod's hand flew out in a swift, sure response, but then hovered uncertainly.

'He doesn't understand the subjunctive yet,' James explained. 'It's got to be a direct command.'

'Oh.' Alex thought for a moment, then tried again. 'Give the micrometer to the Major,' she said.

Hector's hand moved slightly; he'd heard the instruction, but was not proceeding on it.

'He doesn't recognise micrometers or Majors,' James said, beginning to wish that he hadn't suggested the demonstration. 'You have to be very specific.'

'But how?' said Alex, bewildered.

James took over. 'Listen to me, Hector.' Without warning a green light flickered on the indicator panel set into the robot's chest. 'I've got his attention,' James told them. 'Speech response comes later.' Again he addressed himself to the Demigod. 'Do you know what a lab bench is?' Green light. 'On the bench ahead of you and at approximately sixty degrees, that instrument is a micrometer. Across the bench at about eighty degrees, that man is the Major. Pick up the micrometer and give it to the Major.'

The hooked fingers landed delicately on either side of the micrometer and then closed together as Hector estimated the effort needed to grip and lift. Then the arm extended, offering the instrument to Adam.

'Not bad,' said Adam, impressed in spite of himself. James relaxed a little, his relief obvious. Adam reached out to take the micrometer and complete the scenario.

Hector's claw closed without warning. The toughtened glass on the front of the instrument burst and splintered as the metal casing was crushed in around its centre. Adam froze, his hand in mid air, and then took a step back.

'I'm glad you didn't tell him to shake hands with me,' he said.

'That's not the intellect,' James said, annoyed and

embarrassed, 'that's just straight physical feedback. There's some fine tuning to be done on it yet.'

'Evidently,' Alex said drily.

Alone in the lab, James worked with a feeling of growing bitterness. Hector had failed him, had not given him the edge of authority over the Major that he so desperately needed; instead the Demigod had behaved as a bumbling, overpowered child. Now James's major sources of frustration were language and mechanics as Hector repeatedly failed to give the correct responses to his instructions and adjustments.

Hector *would* learn. The random neural flows within his braincase would be shaped and directed, balk or resist as he may; and if he wouldn't develop on his own, he would be forced. Direct imprinting would drag him every step of the way, and to hell with the official caveat that the technique was not to be used until the basic intellect was fully developed.

James ran his fingers around to the back of his head, searching for and tracing the path of the hard bulge that ran from behind his ear to the niche between the skull and the neck sinews. The hair had grown back on the skin around the implant, but the plastic cap was still in place. He took the small button between thumb and forefinger and gave it a half-twist; it unthreaded and he removed it, placing it on the bench and picking up a small metal probe which ended in a jack connection. Pushing the hair aside with his free hand he inserted the jack into the open socket, giving it the opposite half-twist to fix it in place; then, brushing the hair back to cover the buried probe, he moved over to the Demigod and tuned it to imprint mode.

James had mixed feelings about the implant. Its insertion had been a matter of pride to him, but the wave-output that it gave on test had cost him his promotion . . . but no. It hadn't cost him anything. He functioned within and better than his rank – here he was, proving it.

He stepped back. Hector stepped back as well, banging into the bench and knocking a few unimportant objects on to the floor on the opposite side. James lifted a hand, and Hector lifted a hand.

James smiled. Hector stood, unmoving.

'So you haven't managed to get him to speak yet?'

James didn't look up at Adam's question, but simply shook his head. He was slumped on a lay-low in the general living quarters, radiating tense exhaustion. A few unfinished soy biscuits were broken into crumbs on a plate by his side, and he was holding a half-emptied glass of Alex's amber juice. He took another drink, and almost drained it.

Adam was beginning to relax a little. It seemed that his first response to this new technology – that it would create far more problems than it solved – was correct, and that Alex's ploy with his exercise records might not be needed; in which case all that would be required would be to erase the false data and replay the original figures from the tape copy.

'I don't understand it,' James said at last. 'Everything else is coming along fine, and there's nothing wrong with any of the speech circuits – *I* checked them out twice, and I got one of the lab robots to run through them as well, just to make sure.'

'Perhaps he doesn't want to talk yet,' Alex suggested.

'That's not possible,' James said emphatically. 'Anything I want, he wants. He doesn't have the choice at this stage.'

'I don't know,' said Adam. 'It doesn't sound so

ridiculous to me. You told us you'd set up the basic intellect during the first couple of days. If we're talking about a four week schedule there's been plenty of time for him to start building up his own ideas and prejudices.'

'You don't know what you're talking about,' James snapped, and then tried to compensate for his over-hasty response in tones of reason. 'We're not talking about some street-sweeper driven by a cat's brain. Hector's got a brain that's cultured from a human tissue sample.'

'All the more scope for complications.'

'That's not so. Hector's brain started out almost completely clean, and nothing goes in other than what *I* put there. He's got no conflicts, no complications, no self-doubt. There's nothing you could hang a neurosis on at all, no crisis of identity or anything.'

'I don't see how that's possible,' said Adam. 'You're giving information, he's receiving it. That seems to imply a potential for self-awareness on his part, especially if he's been given the capability to sort the information out for himself. And one week is a hell of a short time to get yourself balanced up under those circumstances.'

James pushed himself forward to the edge of the lay-low, his patience and temper fraying in roughly equal proportions. 'It doesn't work like that,' he insisted. 'Problems like those were worked out in the design stages.'

'But you did say that Hector was one of the *first* of the Demigod series?'

'That makes no difference. All the procedures have been tested and checked. Hector can't have an identity problem, because at the moment the only identity he's got is mine.' James paused, and noted with satisfaction that he had his audience without an argument. To be more precise, they had no idea what he was talking about.

James half-turned, and lifted the hair on the back of his head to show them the locked-in probe. 'This is a wave transmitter,' he explained, 'and there's a receiver and resonator linked into Hector's brain. I've had feedback training which lets me control the transmitter's output and channel my thoughts directly into him.'

'So he becomes a copy of you?'

'Not in any real sense – I told you, I can control it. I select out exactly what I want him to have.'

'You can choose what you're thinking about?'

James nodded, and not without a touch of obvious pride.

'I wish I could,' Adam said, aware that he was not being totally flippant.

'I don't understand how it can work,' Alex said.

James hesitated for a moment, and then levered himself to his feet from the divan. 'Come with me to the lab,' he said, 'and I'll show you.'

They fell in behind him as he led the way down the corridor, and Adam couldn't help smiling as he observed that James had pulled himself together in his tiredness at the prospect of being the centre of attention. The last few days had obviously made heavy demands on his abilities and resources, and the shadow of failure depressed and even frightened him. Now that James and his Demigod seemed unlikely to cause the ruin of the isolated happiness that he shared with Alex on Saturn Three, Adam was able to feel some small measure of sympathy – for the man, if not for the robot. He was so obviously a creature of the world that Adam had quit – nervous, ambitious, sick with a desperation to succeed in the hierarchy of an inhuman and unforgiving organisation, now poised and insecure as he hung with probationary status between ranks. Perhaps the confirmation which would be added to his handler's flashes depended on his achievements with Hector; in which case his future was by no means assured, as his lack of accomplishment seemed to indicate a deficiency in the absorption of his training.

The Demigod stood by the lab bench, masses of hastily-jotted notes and cut wire and discarded tubing strewn around him.

'He hasn't moved since I left,' James explained. 'I haven't wanted him to, and he's no will of his own.'

Alex gave a start as Hector drew himself up and began to move across the lab towards them.

'Careful, Captain,' Adam said quickly. 'Remember what I told you.'

Hector stopped in mid-stride, and then subsided back to a balanced stance. His movements were far more assured than they had been on his first excursion only a couple of days before. The robot's hands came up in a brief, inconsequential movement, almost a human shrug; and then he returned to his position by the bench.

'There's no need to worry,' James said. 'He's moving under my instruction, not of his own free will.'

'Only when you transmit a wave pattern?'

'When I choose to transmit, yes.'

'And what about when you're not transmitting? What goes on in his head then?'

'Damn-all, Major,' James said with a smile. 'The braincase is down in his chest.'

Adam and Alex stood well back as James sent Hector on a tour of the lab, negotiating with care around the tanks and the cabinets and neatly avoiding any collisions. The robot paused at several points and its hand reached out, settling around some object and lifting it into the air before setting it down again with delicacy and precision. James watched closely, brows creased into a slight frown of concentration. A muscle in his neck twitched, almost as if he were sub-vocalising Hector's instructions, and his hands made inconsequential little movements in sympathy with the Demigod's manoeuvres.

Hector stopped at the far end of the lab and turned to face them. The clouded glass of the low-pressure bacterial tanks was behind him, their metalled gridiron divisions a framework against which the robot seemed to be measuring himself. He stood, his lens turret sweeping the lab, as if he would claim it all.

'You see,' James said, 'total control and sympathy. None of the shambling and lurching you saw on his first day.'

'It's very impressive,' Alex said. James looked across at her, and seemed to increase a little in stature with her approval. 'But why,' she went on, 'won't he talk?'

James's face fell. 'I don't know,' he said, and flicked his hand in a throwaway gesture of defeat.

The air rang with the keen agony of breaking glass from the far end of the lab, a dead smack followed by shatter and a bursting of water. One of the bacterial tank divisions dumped its contents through its open front, liquids boiling into gases with the release of pressure as they swamped and flowed around the Demigod's body. Hector's claw was raised in an exact imitation of James's dismissive wave, thrust into the now-open panel on the front of the tank.

The contaminated water hit the floor and spread into an instantaneous sheet, and the dog Sally's frightened howls were added to the noise and confusion as she erupted from her hiding-place between the hydroponics tanks and pelted in head-down terror for the lab doors.

'Out, fast,' Adam commanded, and there were no arguments. They piled out into the corridor, Sally struggling through between James's legs and almost tripping him as the doors slammed together.

The corridor lights were blinking on and off in emergency alarm, and there was the distant echo of a siren from the communications room. The dog was off and away before the people had sorted themselves out. Alex felt a concerned touch on her arm, and in the flare of the corridor lights saw that it was from James; then his hand fell away, and on the next illumination he had stepped back.

The chances were that the bacterial soup contained nothing harmful, but the lab was now sealed airtight until this could be confirmed. Whilst none of the experimental bacteria were particularly virulent, there were some which could not only survive out of the tanks but which could cause sickness and irritation if, by some devious means, they found their way into the gut. Adam had once been laid low by such an organism, and he took no pleasure in recalling the experience.

They made their way to the communications room, where Adam shut down the alarms and asked the base computer for a check on the contents of the ruined tank. James said nothing, and met nobody's eye. In the quiet that followed the persistent whine of the siren Alex cut up the output of the lab camera on to the monitor bank, panning and zooming to give a tightly-framed shot of Hector and the damage. The Demigod was frozen as they had left him, his metal claw still poised in its attitude of destruction; but as James saw this image on the screen, the claw dropped swiftly back to the robot's side.

'There's no danger,' Adam said with relief as the computer gave out its report on the visual display. 'All we've got to worry about is a nasty mess and a lost experiment.'

James offered neither excuse nor apology. He stared at the screen with a silent resentment for his unco-operative ally.

'I suppose,' Adam went on, 'that Hector's numerous inhibitions wouldn't prevent him from cleaning up after himself?'

'I'll handle it,' James said tonelessly.

Adam turned to Alex. 'We may as well go,' he said. 'We can leave replacing the experiment until tomorrow – no sense wading through the crap when we don't have to. Not when we've got Hector to do it for us.'

He said it with resignation, but not with any obvious display of humour. If it had been a joke, James might have resented it and found some outlet for his formless and undirected anger; but as a statement of almost-fact it was cold, simple, and barely resistible.

Damn you, Hector, he thought. What are you trying to do to me?

# NINE

Tired as he was, James spent most of the night directing Hector in his mopping-up. He stood with his hands thrust deep into the pockets of his jumpsuit, watching despondently as the robot cleared the broken glass and went over the floor with a bacteriophage enzyme to consume any surviving members of the colony.

The next morning Adam came into the lab and found it sterile and tidy, the only evidence of the previous night's accident being the gaping maw of the empty tank in the far wall. James was asleep, his head cradled in his folded arms where it had subsided as he sat at the bench. Hector was behind him, a silent sentinel.

James awoke with a start as Adam approached, and Hector seemed to shudder in an unchecked sympathetic response. Alex came into the lab at that moment, carrying an insulated container of Tethys sample to replace the one they'd lost. James looked around blearily as he heard her footsteps, and Hector's lens turret swivelled around in perfect synchronisation with the movement.

Adam watched this thoughtfully. James had supposedly proved himself to be competent in the use of the brain link, but he showed a remarkable lack of control in his unguarded moments. Alex seemed not to have noticed the move; she set the sample case down and turned to go back to the freezer rooms for an appropriate bacterium.

James eased off the lab stool, rubbing his eyes. They were ringed and puffy, and there was a stubble around his chin.

'I'm sorry,' he said. 'I must have . . .' Then he

realised that it was perfectly obvious what he must have done, and so he went on, 'I'll go and get a shower. Then I'll come back and have Hector give you a hand with the sample.'

'It won't be necessary,' Adam told his retreating back, but James seemed not to hear him. The doors parted to let the rumpled jumpsuit and its similarly dishevelled occupant through.

Adam wondered about the advisability of being alone with Hector. There was nothing to indicate that the robot was even active, although Adam knew otherwise; but he wasn't prepared to relinquish any part of his station to a piece of inadequate engineering, and so he went on with his work with a wary eye on the metal body. Every now and again he would be surprised by the sharp whine of a servo motor announcing the twitch of a limb, and Adam assumed that James was occasionally broadcasting an unguarded thought of reaction as he showered. These small lapses apart, Hector stayed in place and behaved himself.

Adam boiled off the sample gases and siphoned them into a pressure tank to re-liquify. A mess of rock waste remained on the tray at the bottom of the container, and he lifted this out for Alex to analyse and grade when she returned.

James was back before Alex. The stubble was gone, and his still-damp hair had been combed – altogether he made a far more presentable sight than when he had left. He saw the sample tray and said, 'Hector can take that, Major.'

'Are you sure?' Adam didn't want to be blatantly difficult, and there seemed to be little enough harm in letting it carve up a few rocks; nevertheless, Hector's controlability was an uncertain factor.

'I fed in the procedures as part of basic station orders,'

James said. 'He can handle it, no problem.'

At that moment Alex arrived with the newly-thawed bacterial colony.

'Dump that in tank twenty-eight,' Adam told her, 'and leave the rest to Hector. Apparently he can handle it.'

She smiled, and said 'Okay.' Adam picked up his clipboard with the experiment log sheets and walked out of the lab, shaking his head in a display of amused disbelief.

'You listening, Hector?' James said, and got the green light. 'This is lab procedure 4002, where you get to analyse the residual waste from the surface samples. You remember it?' Green light. 'Okay, there's a laser saw at ninety degrees and nine or ten feet. You know what a laser saw looks like?' Green light. 'All right, go get it. And stop the procedure if there's anything you don't understand.'

Alex put the bacterial fluid through the pump, but found Hector's activity more interesting. He zeroed in on the laser saw and collected it, holding it aloft as his free hand fixed the largest of the rock samples – a spongy, fist-sized boulder – into a vice. Then he shuffled up close and examined the stone from all angles before bringing in the saw and activating the beam.

The yellow stream of coherent waves hit the rock on its edge and sent a shower of loose particles flying, causing James to duck away. Hector had no such worries, his toughened lenses moving in close to the light-blade as he began a meticulous sawing of a rock wafer.

Alex wandered over, her own work forgotten, fascinated by the robot's delicacy and precision.

'Who devised this procedure?' James asked as she came level with the bench.

'My partner. Why?'

'It's inefficient for Hector. *You* may need to take half a

74

dozen slices to get one good one, but he can get it right every time.'

She frowned at the implied criticism, and glanced down at Hector's bright carving. There was a sudden flaring and she fell back with a searing pain of gravel in her eye.

'What's the matter?' James demanded. 'What happened?'

Hector cut the power to the laser saw, and waited patiently. His lenses swivelled to look at Alex.

'My eye!' she said. 'Something got into my eye!' It felt like a handful of grit had been pushed roughly under her eyelid and then rubbed around to scour at the fragile tissues.

'Let me look,' James said, but Alex pushed his hands away.

'Get Adam, please!'

'I don't know where he's gone. There's a stool just behind you, sit down and I'll try to get it out.'

She allowed herself to be guided back on to the seat, but wouldn't let him near her eye. It was beginning to redden as the lid swelled, but the tears that were now running freely did nothing to wash out the sharp-edged intruder.

'If you won't let me near, I can't help you,' James said, and so reluctantly she let him tilt back her head and gently pull apart the lids to expose the troubled eye.

Hector was leaning over her, his claw outstretched. 'No,' she cried out in sudden alarm. 'What's he doing?'

'It's all right,' James said, pushing her down with his free hand. 'Trust him.'

'No, please,' she protested, 'I don't want him to touch me!'

'Stay still or you'll get hurt!'

The claw poised before her eye and the Demigod's

lens turret moved into place behind it, weaving a little from side to side to get the best possible estimate of depth. She saw through a rippling sheet of tears as a hair-thin prong emerged from the tip of one of the claws. She didn't dare to move, with blindness only inches away.

The claw snapped towards her almost faster than she could make out, and she felt something brush the naked surface of her eye. She blinked in a reaction impossible to resist, her lids pulling free of James's gently restraining fingertips; but the claw had gone, and with it the main cause of her distress.

James moved back, as if suddenly aware of their closeness. Her eye was still sore and streaming, but that was nothing more than an after-effect.

'That's much better,' she said. 'Thank you.' And then, to Hector with some embarrassment, 'Thank you.'

'We're here to help,' James said quietly, 'that's all. You don't have to go on fighting us every inch of the way.'

Hector moved aside, and Alex could now see that Adam was standing in the open doorway. She moved over towards him, dabbing at her damp cheek with the sleeve of her jumpsuit.

'I got some rock in my eye,' she explained. 'Hector took it out for me.'

Adam nodded without expression. 'I saw it,' he said.

Alex went off to rinse her eye in clean water, and Adam moved across to James.

'It was damn lucky for you,' he said with quiet control, 'that you didn't make a mistake with that claw. Because if anything had happened to her . . .'

'I wish I could take the credit,' James interrupted, 'but I can't. Anything you want to say now, say it to Hector.'

Adam didn't understand. 'What do you mean? What

76

about the brain link?'

James turned his head, pushing his hair aside. The probe had gone, and the plastic button was back in its place. 'I took it out when I went to shower. Hector doesn't need me – my mistake was in not letting him take over earlier. He's on his own, now.'

Adam looked at Hector, and for a moment it seemed that Hector was returning the gaze. Then the robot turned, and went back to his work.

# TEN

Adam had come to realise with some annoyance that his work around the station was forming a backlog; as long as James and his robot were occupying the lab Adam was inclined to stay away. There was, however, a limit to the occupation that he could find elsewhere in the complex warren of the Saturn Three underground corridors – after checking all the pumps and seals on the trunking and cabling that ran along and under the base's passageways, and having crawled down every narrow gap that he could find beneath grilled floors and behind sectioned walls, Adam had to face the fact that he would at some time have to return to the main work area.

The hyroponics tanks would have to be drained; the plants' nutrient fluids were becoming stale and choked, and he would need at least half a day to lift out the sections of the lab floor which would give him access to the deep waste pits beneath. Of course, with James's help and Hector's strength it might take less than an hour – but no, Adam wasn't prepared to ask. His bitter antagonism towards their intrusion had diminished and become contained, but still he could not fully relax until the robot was considered completely functional and James had no choice but to leave. The uncertain, undisciplined Demigod seemed unlikely ever to replace a member of base personnel, and James, despite his persistence, met nothing but rejection from Alex. As long as Adam could last out the twelve days to the moon's emergence from shadowlock, everything would be fine.

Soon it would be necessary to make a trip out in the

buggy, leaving Saturn Three's protective warmth for the bleakness of the surface. Sample stocks were down, and as this was supposedly an area of Hector's capability it would perhaps be unavoidable that the obtuse giant should be taken along. It seemed likely that he would be little more than an inert passenger; more than two weeks, and James hadn't even got him to speak yet.

James watched dispiritedly as Hector gave all his concentration to the VDU unit before him. The lines of lettering rolled by too fast for James to follow, but Hector's hungry mind took it all in, occasionally stopping the display and questioning with a few sharp, economical taps on the keyboard. Then the base computer would dutifully re-present the information with added support material and Hector, when satisfied, would indicate for it to continue.

'You can read well enough,' James called out. Hector's visual probe pulled away from the screen, and the gimballed turret at its base swung around to bring the eye to bear on James.

'And you can hear well enough, too.' The probe stared levelly, but Hector showed no further reaction. 'So why the hell won't you say anything? You know you can. There are no faults, no reason why you should go on like this.'

After a moment, the gimbals whirred and the turret swung back to the VDU. A claw darted out and punched in the code to clear the still-rolling type and changed over to keyboard display.

NOT YET READY.

James moved across the room to the unit, delight mingling with disbelief to modify his anger and frustration. 'You sly bastard! There's *nothing* wrong with your communication centres, and you let me think you

79

weren't capable!'

FULLY CAPABLE BUT NOT YET READY.

'Why? I mean, why not?'

No response.

'What's stopping you? Is it him? Or is it the girl?'

YOU.

'Me? What am I supposed to have done?'

MURDER.

James stared, bewildered and sick as the whole focus of his life began to shift. The act that he had thought would clear the slate of his competitive failure, an arrangement of events which he had thought were contained in his mind alone and which could be modified into a new truth by persistent self-delusion – this act was now the speculative property of another intellect. Competent, successful probationary Captain-handler James began to crumble and dissolve, leaving the twisted failure Benson in his place.

'Blank that!' he shouted angrily. 'You've got no right to say that!'

BLANKED AS ORDERED.

James breathed deeply, and his world began to fall back into its proper shape. 'That shouldn't have come through the link. What else do you know about me?'

YOU FAILED COURSE.

'Blank that.'

BLANKED AS ORDERED.

'Anything else?' The claw did not move. 'What about the girl?' It hovered, uncertain of its response. 'Are you aware of her?'

AFFIRMATIVE.

'And what do you think?'

BEAUTIFUL.

James laughed, and the turret swung around to look at him.

WHY.

'Take a look at yourself, Hector, and don't get ideas above your station. Ball-bearings are no substitute for the real thing.'

YOU LAUGH – KILLER.

'I told you to get that erased,' James snapped. 'Now blank it!'

BLANKED AS ORDERED.


'So? Am I a killer?'

BLANKED AS ORDERED.

'Don't give me that. I want a straight answer.' The claw hung over the keys. 'So, if you don't think I'm a killer, and you still won't talk to me, you must be malfunctioning . . .'

AM NOT MALFUNCTIONING.

'And if there's nothing wrong in the speech circuits, the fault must be in the brain. That means a flash-burning for you and a new braincase on the next available drop. Is that what you want?'

AM NOT MALFUNCTIONING AM NOT MAL-FUNCTIONING AM NOT MALFUNCTIONING AM NOT MALF.

YOU ARE A.

Hector hammered on at the keys, even though James had cut the power to the VDU and walked away. After a few moments he stopped and was still; then the claw reached over to flick a switch and restore the power. Within a few seconds the screen was again a rolling mass of data as Demigod and base computer conspired together.

# ELEVEN

'I don't think you should be alone with the robot. James ought to go with you.'

'We've been over this,' Adam told her as they moved towards the Central Nucleus. 'It's obvious that the machine's never going to be anything more than a mobile pair of hands, and a pretty inept pair at that. It's never going to say anything and it's certainly never going to replace one of us. The sooner we can say we're satisfied with its basic functions, the sooner we can ship James back to the platform. Then he can drag his tail back to Earth or go singe it on the sun as far as I'm concerned. Once he's gone we can pull the plugs on old Hector and get back to normal.'

She was not reassured. 'It could be dangerous. We've seen what Hector's capable of.'

'He's been fine ever since James took him off the brain link, which is understandable. Anybody with their mind on a direct line to his should be excused a few wild actions.'

James was waiting for them in the Central Nucleus, standing apart from his protégé and displaying a distinct lack of paternal pride. Alex didn't help by asking if Hector had started to speak yet; James actually winced at the question. Alex said a quick goodbye to Adam, and then disappeared before she could be left alone with James.

'I ought to come with you,' James said doubtfully.

Adam smiled, and shook his head. 'You can't wet-nurse him all the time, and I can't delay this trip any longer. Let's see if he's as good as you say he is.'

'He's good. He's got everything but the speech, and that's . . . not really essential.'

'Rather depends on what he's trying to tell you, doesn't it? But my main concern is that he'll be able to understand me.'

'He's got a full vocabulary and he probably knows more about Saturn Three than you do. He's sensitive to the wavelength of your suit radio, so no problem there.'

'Okay.' Adam moved towards the ramp which led to the airlock. 'Let's get suited up and go.'

'I'll come up with you,' James offered, but Adam waved him back.

'May as well start as we intend to continue. Let's get going, Hector.'

'Carry on, Hector,' James said, but Hector was already moving.

James's suit hung in the racks by the airlock door, and Adam eyed it with envy as he struggled into his own, less flexible pressure garment. Hector needed no extra protection against surface conditions, his armoured body drawing its energy needs from the internal power supply that he replenished every twelve hours or less, depending on his requirements.

'Open the door, Hector.' James had fitted most of the internal doors of the station with a manual opening trigger which Hector could operate, circumventing the need for the biocapacitance sensors, but the airlock door was a simple servo control intended for the clumsy grasp of gloved fingers. It should have given Hector no trouble, but he stooped and peered at it with his sensor extended, tapping and probing experimentally with an uncertain claw.

Adam moved forward with his helmet under his arm, and pushed the robot gently aside. The turret whipped round at the unexpected pressure but Hector's legs absorbed the slight unbalancing effect and he moved away.

'You're big,' Adam muttered, mostly to himself, 'But you're not so bright.' As the door opened he led the way through the decontamination chamber into the airlock proper, aware that Hector was following from the swing and clank of his metal tread. Adam fixed the seals on his helmet and tested his airflow as he walked, but when he turned to close the airlock doors he saw that the Demigod was hesitating in the archway, turret swivelled to look back with apparent uncertainty into the main body of the station.

Like a child on his first day at school, Adam thought, and said, 'Come on, Hector. Time to strike out on your own.'

Hector moved on into the airlock, dull gold against grey. The doors clamped together behind him and locked as the base's atmosphere was withdrawn and conserved.

The buggy was charged up and stacked with a selection of quarry grenades, and there seemed barely enough room for Hector to climb aboard in spite of the fact that Adam had left behind some of his usual equipment when he had prepared the vehicle for the expedition. Another black mark for the adaptability of the Demigod series, he thought, and Hector seemed to agree; he eyed the buggy with obvious trepidation, like a maiden aunt considering an offer to go hang-gliding.

'It's perfectly safe,' Adam said, and this seemed to decide Hector. He swung around and marched determinedly back towards the outer airlock door.

Adam voiced an appeal to heaven as he hurried over to the robot and caught it by the shoulder joints. The open articulations were at the same height as his helmet, but they were the only part of the metal colossus that his

84

gloved hands could easily grip.

The threat to his balance stopped Hector. The lens turret motored around, the sensor hanging level with Adam's faceplate.

'Look,' he said, trying to sound reasonable whilst aware of the absurdity of the need, 'you have to get in the buggy. There's enough room and it's easily strong enough to take you. If you don't get in the buggy you can't come with me. And if you don't come with me, the whole thing's off.'

Hector gave the matter some consideration. After a few seconds he consented to turn around and follow Adam back to the buggy.

'*Now* what's the problem?' Adam was halfway into the driving seat, but Hector was still regarding the buggy with deep suspicion.

'Get in.' There was no response.

Damn you, tin man, you're starting to get to me. Adam climbed wearily from his seat and circled the framework of the open vehicle yet again. If Hector wouldn't jump, he'd have to be pushed.

At the first touch the robot's arm whipped aloft and Adam ducked away from the blow, throwing himself back and blocking with his forearm; but the claw quivered as the servos fought each other, equal forces demanding blood and restraint in equal measures.

Adam was safely out of reach, and the robot was not moving to attack him further. The clawed arm was slowly lowered, but the revelation had been made, a brief glimpse into the pit of hungry snakes that was the Demigod's – and, by reflection, it's trainer's – mind.

If it wouldn't come, let it stay. Adam walked back to the driving seat without further comment, but as he did so Hector clambered awkwardly on to the framework and lowered his oversized bulk into the passenger seat. Now

85

it was Adam's turn to hesitate; but then he warily climbed aboard and reached for the remote switch to open the outer doors.

Whenever Adam was out of the base it seemed to Alex that her perceptions of her surroundings underwent a subtle alteration. Lights seemed brighter and harder, and the odd and ordinarily comforting sounds of the station acquired a new and unfamiliar edge. Knowing that James was around did nothing to temper these feelings of disjointed isolation; if anything, his distant presence intensified them. In an attempt to find some small measure of comfort against the chill or loneliness Alex went to look for the only sympathetic life form that was left in Saturn Three.

Sally was in one of her usual places, asleep on top of the heat-exchanger cover. A dark, slightly greasy patch on the white of the insulation betrayed her liking for its warmth and the frequency of her visits. The dog moaned blearily as Alex scooped her off and cradled her, finding some immediate primeval reassurance in the close touch of warm fur. It was a need, an obvious and inexplicable need; as inexplicable as a yearning to see just once, open skies and uncultivated green, and to feel the warm scented wash of freely moving air – the sad dream of the Spaceborn.

She turned, murmuring to the dog of nothing in particular. James was watching her.

'How's the eye?' he said, not managing to make it sound like he wanted to know the answer.

'It's fine. No problem at all.'

He nodded, but didn't seem to have taken the information in. The conversation was nothing more than noise – his mind was elsewhere.

'Put the animal down,' he said abruptly.

'What?'

'Put the animal down.' His tone suggested that he was in some way offended by the display of affection that was being given to what was, in his experience, a meat animal.

'I don't know what's wrong with you,' Alex said, passing him and taking her compliant furry bundle down the ramp towards the main nucleus. James wheeled to follow, and raised his voice as he called after her.

'Wrong with *me*? There's nothing wrong with me. But there seems to be one hell of a mix-up in your priorities, girl.' They came into the general living quarters with James trying to get around Alex to confront her.

'Old men and dogs, that's all you seem to go for. What's so bad about me? What's so bad that I don't rate?'

Alex looked through him, past him, anywhere but at him. She said nothing.

'May I ask you a question?' Still nothing. 'Do you want children, Alex?'

She moved off, and again he followed, still talking. 'Because I'm sure you'll qualify, make the grades easily. But not with him as a sponsor.' She was stalking off along the corridor towards the sleeping quarters, her angry stamping shaking the gridirons of the floor. 'They've got to be choosy about the ones they let through the net,' he shouted, 'and rusty old spacers rate pretty low. You can do better!'

Alex disappeared around the metalled curve of the tunnel. James hurried after.

The buggy had cut yet another pair of irregular ruts into the wide swathe that converged on the entrance to Saturn Three, but on this trip the vehicle had covered no more than the couple of hundred yards to James's spacecraft. As they'd drawn level with the spider-legged structure Hector had reached over and deliberately operated the buggy's hydrogen cut-off, keeping his claw firmly clamped on the handle so that Adam had no choice but to roll to a halt.

'Hector, what do you think you're doing?' Adam demanded, but the robot swung his ponderous legs out of the buggy and pushed himself upright on Tethys's ice-and-rockdust surface. Only a few feet away the gases had swamped and refrozen into a petrified tide, a mirror-molten pool around the spacecraft.

Adam waited a moment, uncertain, but Hector for some peculiar and unfathomable reason of his own did not want to go on the journey. Another failure, and another supportive argument for the status quo; but then, perhaps, another reason for James to extend his stay.

The issue was decided; the trip was under way, and the Demigod had backed out. Adam reopened the cut-out and moved off, unsure of whether to be delighted or depressed.

He risked a glance back before he hit the top of the ridge. The heroic caricature of Hector's body shell had not moved, a headless Talos inhabited by a dark and lonely spirit. Then the buggy threw a wheel into the air, searching for a grip over the knife-edge, and the ridge arose to block the view.

Hector waited for a few seconds longer. The anglepoise apparatus which was mounted on the turret between his shoulders was extended to its fullest, raising the sensory eye to watch for any further sign of movement; and when there was none, the sensor retracted to its normal angle and the robot began a careful turn.

Testing his weight carefully on the ammoniated ice, Hector moved towards the spacecraft. It would be impossible to say whether there might have been sufficient poetry in his unhappy soul to view it as the womb that had carried him in ignorance to Saturn Three, but there can be no doubt that he was fully acquainted with the inter-related complex of parts and principles that made it a working mechanism; it was a mere fraction of the information given to him by the base computer.

The ice cracked and split underfoot, but there was solidity beneath. He came within the shadow of the spacecraft's leg and moved in to locate the maintenance panels for the drive's ignition systems, spreading his skeletal arms wide and forming his claws into the shape of the keyed release tool that would unlock the panels and give him access.

After a few minutes' work amongst the conduits and pressure tubing in the spacecraft's belly he moved around and sought out the communications wiring, tugging lengths of cable free and snipping them neatly before pushing them through the craft's internal spaces on a new routing.

When he had finished, Hector lifted the panels back into place before turning and walking back across the craggy ice towards the seam that was the entrance to the station. This time his claw had no trouble in grasping the servo handle and operating the release mechanism, and once inside the hangar he twisted the mirror-image internal servo to full emergency lock. The heavy door dropped swiftly and in silence, and Hector went on turning in a powerful movement that wrenched the handle out of its mounting.

James caught up with Alex and even managed to get in front of her, hopping backwards as he tried a new angle of attack.

'I'm sorry,' he said. 'I've got no reason to be getting

angry with you. I'm making a fool of myself, I know.'

'Forget it.'

'You know I'm under tension . . .'

'I said forget it.' They were coming level with the sleeping quarters entrance; Alex suddenly wished that she'd given more thought to her route.

'I'm not talking about Hector,' James said, blocking the doorway as the panel slid aside behind him, 'I'm talking about you and me. You've got me so messed up about *nothing* – nothing at all – that I've even ballsed-up Hector's training. And it's your fault, Alex. Back on Earth nobody would even think twice about this but *you* – you hold back and beat me off like I was some grubby kid.'

'I don't want to talk about this,' she said tersely, and tried to push past him. He caught her by the shoulders, and Sally dropped yelping to the ground.

'I'm not trying to cut the old man out,' he said quickly. 'He wouldn't have to know. *You* wouldn't have to know – I could give you a blanker and wipe the whole thing.'

He was strong and intense, and he was holding her, his eyes pleading with her own. The dog was no longer an interfering obstacle between them, and Alex found that she could not longer resist her own impulses as propriety deserted her. She belted James with all her strength, and walked away.

James fell back against the doorway, his head ringing with the blow. The dog was backed off a few feet and barking at him, so he aimed a kick at her. His foot missed but Sally turned and ran, barking all the way.

As Alex emerged into the living quarters she could hear Sally's shrill anger, and it mirrored her own. The sounds of canine temper receded as she scampered off down the corridor that circled the Central Nucleus; in a few seconds the noise would begin to approach, this time from the opposite side of the quarters as the dog came around to complete the circuit.

The noise fell away, moving into transition at the furthest part of the circle, and Alex hesitated as she unconsciously waited for it to resume; then she smiled through her annoyance as she realised what she was doing, like counting the chimes of the clock when you already knew the time. Sally had probably dashed into the lab and made for the sheltering warmth of the hydroponics tanks.

The scream came then, distant but impossibly loud and distressingly short, and Alex began to run. If James had taken out his bitter resentment on the dog she was sure she would kill him, regardless of his size, his strength, or his rank. The corridor seemed to snake on forever, although she knew it was really no distance at all; turning, rising and falling to take account of the folding of Tethys's subsurface structures, branching and broken by doors and offshoots until suddenly she was at the lab.

The doors were wide open. Hector's eye turret spun around to bear on Alex and then he began to turn to her, raising his hands. Look, he seemed to say, I have a gift for you.

What had been Sally was now two pieces of bloody fur and meat, broken and crushed by Hector's tearing grip. His golden armour had been splattered by the small explosion of gore. He took a step towards Alex, holding out his dripping offering, but she backed away; another of the robot's heavy steps and she backed away again, realising too late that she had allowed herself to be pushed out of reach of the lab's only doors.

The Demigod came on, and Alex retreated further, her mind racing. Hector was back in the base when he should have been out with Adam – why? Had Adam given up and abandoned the robot to find his own way home, or was their separation due to some less innocent cause? Hector had torn the dog open and he could easily do the same to a man, pressure suit or no pressure suit. The idea horrified her but she was able, as she backed around the lab, to consider it with logic and clarity. The blood was starting to coagulate on Hector's body shell, forming thick droplets on the clean metal. Tethys's surface was vacuum, and if Hector were to treat a man under those conditions as he had treated Sally in the fifteen pounds psi pressure of the station, the resultant explosion would surely drench him from head to foot with a sticky mess that would resist even the cleansing winds of the decontamination chamber.

The blood on Hector was on his arms and chest, nowhere else apart from where it had run and begun to dry in thin rivers down his legs.

Assuming Adam to be alive, how could she call him? The robot had effectively blocked her off from the door, so she had no hope of making it to the communications room; there was no way that she could even call James, that most unlikely of allies.

She had been pushed over by the bacterial tanks now, as far back into the lab as she could go, and still Hector was moving in slow strides towards her. The door was now impossibly far away but the lab was wide, and Hector was slow; his turret could swivel with speed and his arms could move like whips, but as long as she stayed beyond his reach she could outrun his rocking gait.

If she feinted to his left, she could put the bulk of one of the lab's handling robots between them. The lab robot was like a wheeled spider, bristling with grabs and pincers, and there was even a chance that Hector could get tangled up in it; at the worst he would have to move it aside before he could follow, and then the route to the door was a narrow alley between the lab benches and a number of the other robots stacked against the curving wall. The final obstacle was the massive handling crane, left out of place as James had discarded it when assembling his malevolent child. Hector was big and would manoeuvre with difficulty through this simple labyrinth of furniture and metal, and Alex might even have time to rip James's improvised control box from beside the door, trapping the Demigod in the lab as he laboriously retraced his steps down the open centre.

Closer he came, and she braced her hands on the glass panels of the tank behind her to push for a fraction of extra speed. Then she dived, and was under the sweep of his arms before he realised what she was doing, running for the gap and dodging through it as Hector began his slow turn to follow.

Alex was banged hard against the edge of the bench as her leg was pulled from under her, and as she kicked to regain her balance she found that the spider robot had flicked out an arm and caught a grip on her pants leg. It was a weak arm intended for delicate assembly and she knocked it aside easily, but as she did so another came out and took its place; and as she fought this one, two more.

The supposedly safe path ahead was lined with waving grabs and pincers as the lab robots all became active. Some were microgrips that, even if they could reach her, could give her no more than a playful nip; others could bite through a limb in an easy movement. Hector had commanded them all as they had assembled his body, and he was commanding them now. Alex didn't dare to run their deadly gauntlet, and now Hector had moved into place to seal her into the alley.

She pushed the spider robot free and launched it at

Hector's legs, realising the futility of the action as she did so; the spider was a light alloy on rubber wheels, enough perhaps to trip a man but nothing to worry Hector's metal mass. The spider bounced from his shin and spun as he stepped over it, clearing it out of his way with a savage backward kick.

The spider skittered out of control across the jointed panels of the lab floor. It came up hard against the ground-level glass of one of the tanks, and was immediately pushed away by the outrush of boiling fluids as the glass gave way and the contents dumped in a re-enactment of an earlier accident.

Hector's turret swung around at the noise, away from Alex. Although the spillage offered him no threat it seemed that he looked on it for longer than was necessary, perhaps remembering his indignity under James's imperfect control.

Alex saw her chance, and jumped on to the lab bench by her side. There was a mass of wire and packing material on it that she swept away as she scrambled across, diving for a headlong fall into the open space at the far side. Hector's right claw shot out and closed around her wrist.

James was in the Central Nucleus as the lights began to flash in the bacterial alert signal. He looked around in confusion for a moment and then began to move, slowly at first, towards the lab. As his confusion cleared he began to run, and when the lab doors zipped open and he sprinted through he nearly fell as his foot slid across drying blood.

He steadied himself as he looked down the lab. Hector was holding Alex with a claw around each wrist. The robot had nearly hoisted her into the air, and her contact with the floor was obviously slight; he had brought her almost level with his sensory eye, and this hovered before her face.

'Hector,' James said, trying to muster a tone of confident command, 'put her down.'

The eyestalk moved aside for a moment, taking him in. Then it motored back to Alex.

The buggy nearly took off as it hit the ridge and bounced on to the long slope for the last stage of the return to the station. Adam had been out of the vehicle for some time and so had no idea how long the red alarm light had been glowing on the dashboard, Saturn Three's quiet cry of danger. It could be an accident, it could be a fault, or it could be an improvised plea for help. He boosted his helmet radio receiver to the top of its power, putting his life-support systems at risk, but there was no broadcast from the com room, no easy reassurance from Alex that everything was under control.

The rover bucketed down the slope much faster than safety allowed, but somehow it managed not to turn over. Hector was gone from his place by the spacecraft, and a suspicion began to form in Adam's mind; a suspicion accompanied by a deep-seated horror at his own lack of anticipation.

The automatic door release failed to respond, and Adam levered himself out of the buggy to lumber over and see if there was any reason. Nothing was visible. But without access through this outer door he was effectively barred from the station.

He felt a growing panic at being held back, but he concentrated and tried to channel it into productive energy. One of the red quarry grenades would easily take out the entire door, but these were all in the rack on the upper nucleus. All he had with him were blues, effective enough in their own way but not sufficient to make a hole in metal.

He thought for a moment, keenly aware that valuable seconds were slipping away. Then he returned to the buggy and heaved out a filled sample case, the only one that he had loaded before seeing the alarm signal. He carried it over and set it down by the deep seam that marked the door's side channel before returning to the buggy. This time he came back with three of the blue grenades, setting them down by the case before turning to it and breaking open the pressure seal on its lid.

The ice crystals in the case were like black salt, ammonia and methane locked at low temperature with a rocky shrapnel. Adam took two of the blue grenades and laid them in the seam, bedding them into place with handfuls of inky snow. When he was satisfied with their placing he packed chunks and crystals from the sample case all around the cylinders, and then picked up the remaining grenade and moved back to the buggy.

The grenade was mainly a close-work tool, not intended to be aimed with accuracy over any distance. Adam rested it on the chassis of the buggy and tried without much confidence to sight along its length.

Grey steam erupted from the nozzle in a concentrated slug, arcing through vacuum and expending itself in a wispy cloud against the door, a couple of feet in from the edge.

The gases in the crack began to boil off as the heat of the metal spread to them. Adam quickly re-sighted and fired again.

The grenades caught and erupted, gases bellying out in a widening cloud of silence. Adam could feel through his suit as fist-sized rocks battered the frame of the buggy as he crouched behind it, and only when the vehicle stopped shaking and juddeing did he raise his faceplate to take a look.

The sidewall had been partially excavated, and the edge of the door had been bent outwards. There was just sufficient room to pass through.

*

'I know what it is,' James said, advancing a couple of steps but not daring to go any closer. 'I think I know what's wrong.'

'Don't keep it to yourself,' Alex said, unable to take her eyes away from Hector's hovering sensor.

'He won't listen to me, but he might to you. Try him.'

'What . . . what should I say?'

'Ask him to put you down.'

Her toes were barely on the floor, and the agony in her wrists was intense. 'Please, Hector,' she said, 'put me down.'

There was a pause, and then the pain began to ease. She was slowly being lowered, the strain on her arms diminishing as she found her footing again.

'Why is he doing this?' she asked helplessly. 'What's wrong with him?'

James was holding back, not wishing to antagonise Hector. 'He learned too much from me. I wanted you, he wants you – but he doesn't know why or how.'

The pincerlike hands opened, and Alex dropped free. Her legs refused to support her and James moved in quickly to catch her before she fell, pulling her back out of Hector's reach and half-carrying her towards the lab doors. The robot's eye turret followed him.

'It's all right,' James said soothingly as he stroked Alex's hair. 'We'll just back up slowly and get out of the lab. He doesn't really want to hurt you.'

'He's got a damn funny way of showing it.'

The crane arm smashed down on to the lab bench, metal screaming in protest at the sudden strain. The foamed plastic top split across the middle as all the equipment on it sprang into the air; cabling to the power points jerked free and the massive concrete blocks that formed its base began to totter and fall as the crane itself overbalanced and leaned into the wreckage.

James barely had time to push Alex clear before he

was overtaken by the tide of heavy debris. The upper girder of the crane swung free as it dropped, sweeping across James's leg and upending him as the tabletop crashed on to the floor. At the far end of the lab Hector's arm was raised, fingers closed in a grotesque skeletal parody of a fist.

'I'm trapped,' James said wonderingly. There was no feeling in his leg, but it wouldn't pull out of the ruin of the crane. Alex was pushing herself into a sitting position on the floor a few yards away, dazed and confused.

'Get me out,' James pleaded. 'You must get me out! I can't stay in here with *him*!'

James, Alex, Hector – all three swung around in surprise as the lab doors flew open. Adam stood, his helmet gone but otherwise still dressed for the surface, breathless and panting from his run through the nucleus. Behind him the corridor lights still pulsed their alarm, and the distant whine of the com room siren added its keen edge in the hiss and crackle of severed wiring within the lab.

He saw Alex on the floor and Hector, immobile, some distance beyond. Without hesitation he moved to her and pulled her up on to her feet, half-carrying her to the doorway and propelling her through.

'Leave him,' she said as he turned back for James.

'I'll be all right,' Adam assured her.

As he moved towards the wreckage of the crane, Hector started forward. James began to scream for help, terrified that Adam would back off and desert him, but Adam started to clear the various lab benches on to the floor in the robot's path. Wire, cable, delicate instruments, heavy apparatus – all were heaped into an improvised barricade to slow Hector down. A couple of the lab robots came for him but he sidestepped and upended them, adding their mass to the debris.

98

Hector hit the low obstruction and started to wade through. He was immensely strong but his steps were short and he was able to make little clearance from the ground, so that after the first couple of paces his feet became tangled and his balance was threatened.

Adam pulled at one of the bracing struts from the shattered bench. It came free with difficulty, and he inserted it under the crane arm that was pinning James's leg and tried to lever it upward. Hector was shuffling on, making slow progress but managing to shake himself loose to some extent. The arm lifted a couple of inches and James began to drag himself free.

Hector kicked hard, ripping his way through several loose coils of cable and heaving a great weight of junk with him as he brought the other leg over to follow. Adam let the crane arm drop as James's foot slid from under, grabbing a double handful of the collar of his jumpsuit and lifting him bodily. James made for the door with Adam supporting him as Hector rid himself of the last of the detritus with another savage kick and stepped out to cover the short distance remaining.

Alex was holding the doors, her hand over the bio-sensor. James was pushed roughly through the opening as Adam turned and grasped the makeshift servo box that James had installed for Hector, dragging it loose and flinging it into the corridor so that the Demigod would have no chance to reconnect it.

Hector was upon them as the doors slammed together. There was a thump from within the lab as he hit the panelling and then, after a pause, an angry drumming.

James was where he had fallen, hunched in the angle between wall and floor on the far side of the corridor.

'How long will the door hold?' he asked.

The drumming slowed, became a regular, hard pounding.

'Depends how strong that maniac machine is,' Adam replied. 'Let's get to the com room where we can see what he's doing.'

Nobody offered to help James, but he was able to limp along on his own a few yards behind. 'It's not just the strength we have to worry about,' he said, 'he's got a mind, as well.'

'Yes,' Alex said coldly. 'Your mind.'

Alex killed the com room siren as Adam activated the monitor screens, punching a view of the lab through the vision mixing panel to appear on the main screen. The doors came into view, concave and dented but as yet unbreached. Hector was nowhere to be seen. Then he came into shot, holding something shapeless and difficult to identify which he pressed up against the biosensor.

'Sally,' Alex said.

The sensor gave no response, and Hector dropped the piece of dog to one side. It left a bloody mark on the wall. He lumbered closer to the sensor, seemed to be trying to push himself close to it.

'Trying to use his brain mass to trigger the doors,' Adam said.

'Can he do that?'

Adam shrugged. The doors did not move. The robot's bodyshell was too much of a shield. He moved away, and within moments was back with the strut that Adam had used to free James – or, at least, something very like it. He inserted it into the edge of the left-hand door and hauled on it, but the strut bent easily in the middle and this too was thrown aside.

'What kind of emergency procedure have we got to fall back on?' Adam demanded of James.

'I don't know.' James seemed to be drained of all arrogance and self-assertion, his eyes locked to the monitor screen. 'If we weren't in eclipse, we could call up the Survey.'

'But we've got another six days of shadowlock to look forward to. Think of something else.'

Hector was back again, this time carrying the laser saw.

'He can't be stopped,' James said. 'He goes on and on. He's one of the Demigods.'

The laser burned for some time before Hector cut the power and moved in to check his progress. The seam where the doors met was blackened and scorched, and as the camera iris opened up after its initial reaction to the brilliance of the laser it was possible to make out a definite irregular gap.

Hector dropped the laser and reached out with both claws, gripping the tortured metal and exerting a steady pull. Nothing happened for a few moments and then, slowly, the panel began to bend inwards. The robot braced himself and pulled again; the panel bent further, a little less this time.

'Is it my imagination,' Adam said, 'or is he getting tired?'

James took a renewed interest. 'I think he's getting low on charge,' he said. 'Kill the power and we might have him.'

'Kill the power and we kill ourselves. This is Tethys, not Earth.'

Hector's latest effort on the door had got him almost nowhere. He took a few paces back, and his turret scanned around the lab. Then his claw came up and removed the cover from his power receptor as he moved over to the assembly bench.

'We've got to stop him,' said Alex.

'No.' Adam was starting to get an idea. 'Let him go ahead.'

'But you could cut the power from here.'

'He'd find a way. We've no control over the power supply to the hydroponics or the bacterial tanks – he could drain off one of them.'

'But we can't let him recharge,' James cut in. 'He'll be out of the lab within minutes if we do.'

'We can't stop him, but we can overload him.' Adam moved to the racks at the back of the com room. The power routings of all the free sockets in Saturn Three were here, connected and set by a cross-patching of cables and u-links. 'I'll give him a headache he won't forget. Just tell me which socket he goes for.'

Hector had moved out of shot, and Alex operated the rocker control to track him. He came into frame with his back towards the camera, unravelling the single feed wire for the recharge.

'He's blocking the view,' Alex said. 'He's going for one of the sockets in the assembly area, but I can't tell which.'

Hector bent forward, claw outstretched.

'I'll play safe and boost them all,' Adam said, busily re-routing. 'Just tell me when.'

'But I don't know! I can't see!'

'Now!' James said urgently as Hector began to straighten, and Adam threw the handle to complete the routing.

Hector reared up, arms straight down and the jointed bearings of his spine bent into a backward arc, sparks dancing around his chest as the unfused wire began to smoke and burn. Other equipment in the lab was blowing as well at the indiscriminate overload; then the wire burned completely through and Hector fell.

There was a bitter odour of electrical fire easing through the gaps in the shattered door. Adam placed a cautious hand over the sensor. The undamaged half of the door slid open whilst the other lurched a couple of times before jamming completely.

Hector lay where he had fallen. The lab was in semi-darkness – most of the auxiliary lighting had been run through free sockets to be placed where it was most needed. Even so, it was possible to see that Hector was totally inert and unmoving.

'He's out,' James said, somewhat unnecessarily. He balanced on his bruised leg and aimed a kick at Hector's side with the other. 'You'll get no more trouble from him.'

'Or from you. As soon as we're out of eclipse I'm making a report on this. Before that I want you off the base.'

James glanced involuntarily at Alex, and Adam noted the action. 'You can't do that. Not before I've completed.'

'As far as I'm concerned, you've completed.'

'You think that's how Demigods are *supposed* to be? There was a fault, a mistake somewhere, that's all . . .'

'That's *all*?'

'There's a procedure for anything like this. Survey will send us a new braincase and we'll start all over again.'

'Like hell we will. Get Hector broken down and get off my base.'

'It's alive!' Alex said in sudden alarm, and both men looked towards Hector as she pointed.

The pincer twitched, the arm moved an inch or so, the sensory eye quivered a little on its stalk.

Adam's foot came down hard on Hector's claw as James fell heavily on to the robot's chest, reaching for the lens turret and forcing it aside as he sought the release lever between the shoulders. Hector began to move with a little more strength, jerking his claw free and reaching blindly for James; Adam fell to his knees and caught hold of the metallic forearm, trying to wrestle it back to the ground as it powered against him. James had unlocked the turret mechanism but was having trouble with the airtight seal on the braincase access, his fingers scrabbling without purchase on the recessed lock which would need a full half-turn before it would open.

James and Adam both hit the floor and rolled as Hector came bolt upright, limbs threshing to fight off unseen enemies. His eye turret swung freely as he groped behind him to find some means of levering his bulk off the floor. He found the assembly bench, grasping its edge and using his slowly increasing energy to pull himself up, legs rigid and outspread to act as pivots; but then James hurled all his weight against Hector's right leg and the metal heel skidded and lost grip on the lab floor. The claw was pulled free and Hector fell backwards, floor panels shaking at the impact.

Again Adam tried to contain the robot as James crawled around to get a better angle on the braincase. Adam found he was being lifted without much difficulty as he tried to pin down both of Hector's arms.

'Hold him for a couple of seconds,' James said breathlessly, 'that's all I need.'

Adam started to reply but then thought better of it. Hector's control was improving as he shook off the effects of the overload and began to make use of the power he'd absorbed. His claws were snapping like those of some vicious crab, except that these closed with the force of a hydraulic clamp.

Adam lost the robot's right arm, felt it sliding from under him. There was nothing he could do about it, and he tried to shout a warning to James but it was too late; the pincers reached for him, closed on empty air only inches before his face, reached again.

James fell back with the braincase plate in his hands,

and Hector stiffened. His claw stopped in mid-air and then slowly began to subside, settling with the rest of the body as all systems became undirected and slack.

Now that an approach had no danger, James reached into the open neck shaft and lifted out the braincase. Adam allowed himself to slide off the bloodied golden curve of Hector's body shell.

'That's right,' he said as soon as he was able, looking to where James sat on his haunches with the Demigod's braincase cradled in his hands, 'and don't think you have to stop there. I want this thing dismantled piece by piece. Put everything back in the crates and go back where you came from.'

'Survey orders say . . .'

'I'm not interested in what Survey orders say.'

'That's it,' James said, holding the braincase close to his chest as if to protect it from threat or damage, 'whatever you don't like, run away from it.'

Alex had come forward to help Adam to his feet, but he waved her back. 'What I like or don't like has nothing to do with this,' he said. 'If your Demigod had got his way there would have been three people dead here instead of a dog.'

Not three, thought James, and then said, 'You can't go on running your own private world here forever. You turned your back on Earth and now you'll turn your back on progress.'

'If progress is men like you and machines like Hector . . . well, yes, Captain, you're getting the message at last.'

The lab lights were low as the burnt-out units awaited replacement. The blood had been cleaned away and most of the damage had been, if not repaired, at least tidied up. James had done his share in silence, and neither Adam nor Alex had seen any reason to speak to him other than to give brief directions over the placing of some unfamiliar item.

Now Hector lay against the wall, empty of life and drained of fluids, slumped and half sitting with an arm outstretched, its secret works exposed in a process of dissection.

The shoulder joint had somehow managed to tighten itself with use. James had already come to resent Hector, and now it seemed that even his cadaver conspired to anger and frustrate him.

'You want to kill me?' he muttered, leaning hard on the wrench to free the joint and then cursing as it slipped, skinning his knuckles on the moulding of the case. 'Go ahead, kill me.' He reapplied the wrench. 'Or did you want the girl more?' The wrench turned, and the joint began to loosen. 'Now, what could you want with a girl? Or let me be more specific. What could a girl possibly want with *you*?'

The joint opened. James dropped the wrench and gripped the arm with both hands. It remained attached by delicate loops of wire and tubing that really needed careful disconnection; but James pulled savagely, the body shell scraping a couple of inches along the wall before the contacts ripped and parted and the arm came free.

'I needed you, Hector,' he said, and cracked the arm sharply on the edge of the workbench. 'Look what you did to me.'

# TWELVE

'How long before he goes?'

Adam stared into the darkness above the bed and considered the question. 'I don't know,' he said at last. 'He's been working for hours to get the robot dismantled. I don't particularly want to ask him.'

'I know what you mean. At first I thought it was just me being hostile, but . . . well, there's definitely something wrong with his mind, isn't there?'

'Something, I don't know what. All Hector did was to pick it up and act it out. Things must have changed back at the Survey – when I was on the platform somebody like James would have been screened out by the mental tests. God only knows how he ever got to come down here on a mission alone.'

There was a silence. 'He's a killer, isn't he?'

'We've no reason to assume that.'

'I mean, he's capable of it. If Hector tried to do it, James must have thought about it.'

'They're probably all capable of it back on Earth. I wouldn't be surprised if it isn't even against the law anymore.'

Another silence. Then: 'Earth's not really a good place to be, is it?'

He shook his head slowly, and the movement communicated to her. 'A place like that breeds men like him,' he said.

'Is that why you left?'

'I didn't just leave. James was right, and I'm not ashamed of it. I ran.'

Saturn Three, the last sane corner of the solar system.

It was a frightening thought, a fragile situation. Alex found that her urge to leave it had diminished considerably over the period of James's stay.

'Give us a couple of weeks,' she said. 'It will be like nothing had ever happened.' She almost sounded as if she believed it.

Adam sat up suddenly as the door to the sleeping quarters slid open. The corridor outside was at night-light level, and James stood in silhouette.

'These are private quarters, Captain,' Adam said angrily. 'You're out of line.'

'I'm leaving.' As Adam's eye's adjusted to the corridor's light he was able to see that James was in his pressure suit, unzipped and open to show the grimy coverall that he had been wearing to dismantle the robot. 'I'll be taking the girl with me.'

'I'm ordering you out. For the last time.'

'Face it, Major, you're over the hill, inadequate. She doesn't need an old man like you to give her disappointment every night. Let's say I'm relieving you.'

Adam slid out of the bed, came half on to his feet. 'I warned you, Captain . . .'

'I heard you, Major. Twenty years ago you might have been able to make me listen.'

James made a good target, standing in sharp outline, and he failed to hear Adam's barefoot approach. He reached into his coverall but too late; Adam's weight bore him backwards on to the corridor floor, hands around his throat gripping and blocking his air. They sprawled half in and half out of the room, Alex shouting, 'Stop it! Adam, you'll kill him!'

The Captain's skull banged hard against the floor a couple of times. After the first hard blow he stopped resisting but Adam went on, lifting and pounding, until Alex got to him and caught hold of his wrists. He allowed himself to be restrained, releasing James and letting him fall back; then, as the panting animal withdrew and the man took over, he moved back in numb horror.

A place like Earth breeds men like James. And Adam – but Adam runs and won't admit it.

She had draped a robe around his shoulders and was leading him over to the bed. He sank on to its edge and covered his face with his hands as she put her arm around his shoulders and said, 'It's all right. You couldn't help it.'

The wrench flashed in the darkness only inches before her eyes, and Adam immediately went limp and began to slide from her arms. She tried to hold him but he was a dead weight, pulling free and dropping to the floor as she dragged at the robe.

James's hand was on her arm. The wrench was in his other hand, its edge dirtied by blood and hair. 'Time to go,' he said.

'I'm going nowhere with you. Get your hand off me!'

He tightened his grip and hauled her to her feet. 'It's what you want, isn't it? You don't have to lie to please him any more, you're with me now.' He dragged her into the corridor, somehow managing to ignore her struggles as they approached the first intersection of the tunnel.

'Don't even *touch* me!' she said, and finally managed to pull free, falling with the effort.

He turned, and stretched his hand out towards her. 'I'll do what the hell I want with you,' he said, 'and you'll do as you're told!'

He started to step forward, and the pincers closed on his arm a couple of inches above the wrist. He stared at them in perplexity and then in alarm as they began to close, compressing the bones of his forearm together and biting deep into skin and muscle with their hard metal edge. Then a wet click, and the complete hand fell free and spurting.

Hector stepped out of the side-tunnel and caught James as he fell, wrist still clamped aloft to stop the flow of blood. The Captain was lifted into the air as Hector straightened. His eye turret scanned the corridor for a few seconds, lingering on Alex as she tried to make herself as small as possible against the wall; then abruptly he turned and moved off with his unconscious burden.

She watched him go, turning some way down in the general direction of the lab. James's hand lay a few feet away, neat and lifelike as if its separation were some illusion. She got to her feet and ran the short distance back to the sleeping quarters.

Adam groaned as she flicked the room lights on. He was sitting up, gingerly touching a fold of his robe to the back of his head. It came away with a superficial imprint of blood, no more. He looked up at her, eyes focusing with difficulty; and then, as the memory returned, he looked beyond her for James.

Quickly, she told him what had taken place in the corridor. He thought for a moment, then threw the bloody robe aside and moved across to the closet.

'James told us he'd broken that thing down,' he said. 'Maybe he was lying.'

'I don't know why. He was in as much danger as us.'

'I wouldn't care to try explaining how his mind works. All I know is that we can't be safe as long as Hector's prowling the base. We have to get out and away from him.'

'The buggy?'

Adam shook his head. 'He could follow us. And if he didn't, where could we go? The only way out is in the Captain's ship, which means we've got to get to our pressure suits and the airlock.'

'That's right over the other side of the nucleus!'

'You said it.

The shattered door of the lab was now curled back to make an opening wide enough and high enough for Hector to pass through. The lab robots waited in an obedient line, fresh and eager from their recently-completed task of reassembly; but now that Hector was whole again he had no need of them.

They moved back to let him pass. Their minds were dim, barely worth the distinction of the term, but they had the bare minimum of intellect needed to respond to the Demigod's scream from the darkness and their work, once learned, was fast and accurate.

He laid James on the bench, arranging his limbs carefully. The symmetry was spoiled by the lack of a hand, besides which the open arm was beginning to pump and mess up the bench – but it didn't really matter. Not for long.

James's eyelids flickered. His skin was grey, his breathing hoarse and laboured.

'You want to kill me?' James said, but the sound came from Hector. It was low, almost a whisper, not wishing to be heard. 'Go ahead, kill me.' The Demigod took hold of James's remaining complete arm and lifted it, limp and slack. He ran his claw delicately along the upper arm to the shoulder joint, testing for flexibility. 'Or did you want the girl more? He found the pivotal point close to the surface underneath the muscle, and pulled. The cartilage ripped, the joint began to loosen. 'Now, what could you want with a girl?' There was resistance from the sinews, they seemed to stretch and hold where the muscle parted easily. Hector squeezed at the joint with his restraining claw, shearing through the tissues and feeling as they sprang apart with a moist crackling sound.

'Let me be more specific.' The arm came free and he banged it hard on the edge of the bench before laying it aside. 'What could a girl possibly want with *you* now?'

The other arm was much easier. Laying it next to the first, Hector moved around to the head of the bench.

There was no way of telling how long Hector might occupy himself in the lab. They tried to see what he was doing on the Commander's spy-eye monitor in the sleeping quarters, but even on infra-red there were no more than dim shapes visible as the camera tube had overloaded along with much of the other equipment.

They needed to get to the suits and the airlock on the upper nucleus, which meant that they had to reach the upward-sloping ramp. Central Nucleus was the most obvious and direct route, but it would take them perilously close to the lab. Other tunnels could take them on a wider pass, but if Hector decided to come looking for them the slight time advantage would be lost.

The Central Nucleus was empty, innocent in appearance. They crossed it, making as little sound as possible, and entered the corridor which would end in the ramp.

'Oh, no,' Alex said, and Adam threw out a hand to hold her back. Hector had stepped out ahead of them, gleaming soft and golden in the tunnel's low light.

'This way,' Adam said as Hector stepped out towards them, and he hustled Alex back towards the nucleus. Hector was following in silence, his walk betraying none of his earlier uncertainty; perhaps that had been no more than an act.

Several of the tunnels converged on this central area. Alex waited as Adam went back a short distance to check on Hector's progress.

Adam leaned out from the curve of the corridor, ready to dodge an outstretched claw or to turn and run if the Demigod was too close. He saw nothing, leaned a little further.

The tunnel was empty. He turned and ran back to the nucleus. Alex was waiting, watching for his return and so could not see that Hector was emerging into the nucleus only a few yards behind her, striding purposefully forward and reaching out.

To shout a warning, or to stop and try to pull Alex away – there was no opportunity for either of these courses of action. Adam opted to keep on running, grabbing Alex and snapping her round. She gave an abrupt squeak of surprise as she saw Hector's closeness and then they were past, making the best use of the robot's inability to make fast turns.

Hector made no signs of dismay, no futile gestures of frustration. He paused almost thoughtfully, inwardly rehearsing the mechanics of the evasion. He would not be caught in such a manner again. He scanned the tunnels leading off from the nucleus, chose one, followed it.

'I know where he can't follow,' Adam said as they ran along a section where the tunnel humped to follow Tethys's strata.

'Where?'

At the uppermost part of the bulge there was a gap between wall and floor where the preformed sections did not meet. There was barely enough room to squeeze through and crawl into the cableway that ran beneath the floor.

There was light, a fine checkerboard filtered by the grating above. The even blocks of squares spilled and stretched over the bunched cable and tubing, a geometric warping that made it seem that they had been pressed from a single sheet of squared plastic. The clearance was small, and Adam and Alex wormed through with difficulty.

Adam hoped that he would be able to remember his way around the station when seeing it from this unusual perspective. It was fortunate that he had been under the floors only a few days before when checking the pumps that were part of Saturn Three's life-support. If they didn't attract Hector's attention they might even make it as far as the ramp without emerging and risking capture.

At the first intersection Adam reached back and touched Alex, warning her to be quiet and still. Hector was approaching, and even if he did not hear them there was a slim chance that he might detect a movement through the grating.

Hector turned the corner, came towards them. From this angle he looked more massive and dangerous than ever. They held their breath as he lumbered up and right over them, the floor section actually sagging a little as his weight bore down on it; then he had moved on, and Alex let out her breath in a sigh of relief.

Hector stopped. His eye turret swung around – they could see its shadow ripple across the pipes only a few feet from them – probing, searching and then, very slowly, lowering. He moved back, scanning through the floor, and came to stand over them.

He looked at Alex, and then he looked at Adam. Then he took a step back, and reached down.

Adam saw the prongs of the claw pass through the open grill and close in a grasp. 'Move it! he shouted to Alex, and started to scramble backwards as the entire floor section was lifted and the corridor light spilled in. Hector held the section up and leaned in with his free claw, reaching and snapping, trying to get a hold on flesh, cloth – anything that would enable him to drag one of them back.

They were barely out of reach, and Adam had to pull his legs in fast as he felt the brush of the claw on his shin. The robot reacted immediately, returning and snatching, but his target had moved.

The Demigod was at a disadvantage; stooping and lifting complete floor sections made little demand on his strength but gave him difficulties of balance, and the need to be close to the grating restricted his vision. Furthermore, he could only lift one section at a time, and would have to drop it back into place before he could walk across it and raise the next.

Adam and Alex were still moving, following the course of the tunnel. Some stretches were quite open and most of the heavy cables could simply be pushed aside to make a bigger gap. Only the rigid conduits which carried water and steam offered any real problem; some of them went straight across their path, cutting into and through the tunnel wall on either side, and they had to be negotiated with care.

The next intersection was coming up, and Adam hoped that he would be able to remember which way to turn. He tried to visualise as he crawled, imagining the tunnel as it had appeared before they had gone underground. Come on, he told himself angrily, this is the place where you spend every day of your life. You mean to say you've never really looked at it before?

The panel above bent as Hector caught up. The section ahead lifted abruptly and they almost ran into the claw that appeared in the shaft ahead of them. Almost immediately the claw withdrew and the section was dumped back into place, and Adam could see Hector's outline, fragmented by the grating, as he quickly reached for the next panel.

Hector lost a couple of seconds in striding forward, by which time Adam and Alex were under him. They already knew that he would be unable to reach very far underneath the panel that he was standing on, and to have moved in the opposite direction would have entailed a risk of being swept into some dead end.

The panel slammed down, and Hector stepped on to it and turned. 'Time to back off,' Adam said.

Four evenly-spaced conduits blocked their way, horizontal bars with only inches between them. Adam wasted no time with expressions of dismay but wormed across to where the conduit met the wall, eyes straining at the broken patches of light, looking for a joint of a seam in one of the thick tubes. Alex got the message, worming her way to the opposite wall to do the same.

A groove ran around the third pipe, a tight fitting that was almost invisible. He took hold of the pipe in both hands; it was hot but not unbearable, obviously one of the steam conduits. He started to call over to Alex, asking her to see if there was a shut-off handle at the far end of the pipe to cut the supply of steam as he moved it aside; but then he thought better of it, taking hold and twisting to undo the joint.

The conduit broke away from the wall, and steam immediately poured out and began to back up around him. Alex wasted no time in sliding through the gap that the loose pipe had created, but instead of following, Adam manhandled the open end around and thrust it up against the grating. The underfloor channel was already filled with a thick, uncomfortable fog and now this started to boil up into the passageway around the robot.

Alex turned back to look for Adam. All she saw was a grey-white nothing, a damp and sticky swirl that obscured everything beyond a couple of yards.

Adam crawled through the gap in the pipes and tried to see around him. He'd reached the intersection, he could guess that much; but out of three possible directions, which had Alex taken?

Hector turned around in the steam. Condensation was beaded all over his body and on the lens of his eye turret, and there was no way he could wipe it off. He shook the mechanism from side to side, and it re-clouded almost immediately.

Squirming through another gap between wall and floor, Adam raised his head into the corridor and looked around, ready to pull back at the first sign of danger. The fog was still pumping from the side-tunnel a few yards down, but here it was no more than a light mist that threw haloes around the corridor lights.

The ramp was ahead, but Alex was nowhere around. Adam hoped that she'd had a better sense of direction than he, and that she was making towards it. He eased himself out through the irregular crevice with as little noise as possible, although the loud gush of the steam around the corner seemed likely to cover everything. The floor and the walls were wet, and the air was uncomfortably cold against his skin after the stifling confinement of the cableway.

He moved towards the ramp, staying well back from the steaming tunnel mouth. No claw erupted out to grab him, and so he moved on, turning and backing away to keep it in his sight, ready to run if Hector should appear.

No Hector, but Alex stepped uncertainly from a side-branch about a hundred yards back in the direction of the Central Nucleus. She looked around and then saw Adam; her relief was obvious, and she started to move towards him.

Adam touched his finger to his lips in an exaggerated motion of silence. Her run slowed to a walk as she glanced around, and Adam pointed to the nearer side branch that was still pumping steam.

The Demigod emerged from the dense cloud, his timing perfect. The smooth metal of his body shell was glistening and wet, and droplets flew as he shook his eye turret hard from one side to the other. Then he seemed to do a double-take, looking first at Alex and then at Adam as if unable to believe his good luck.

They were far apart, the robot between them. Adam took a step forward, and Hector moved to intercept him. 'Get to the ship,' Adam called, hoping that, given a choice, Hector would want first to ensure his elimination. Alex hesitated. 'Do it! I'll keep him busy!'

Hector's turret swivelled, looked towards Alex. She turned and ran into the tunnel from which she'd emerged, and Adam waited until Hector had wheeled around to look at him again before he turned and started off. Even then, he hesitated before moving out of the line of the robot's sight, wanting to be sure that the Demigod was following.

Hector was advancing steadily, claws raised and half-ready. Adam ran on, made a sharp turn, ducked around the corner and waited. He didn't want Hector to lose him; he had to stay just out of reach, leading the robot on and buying time for Alex. Then he would have to think of some strategy for himself, but at the moment he considered this to be of lesser importance.

He seemed to have been waiting for an uncomfortably long time. He leaned out, ready to pull back at the first sign of danger, wary at first and then, as the wide empty corridor stretched before him, confused.

'Hector!' he shouted. 'Where are you? Come and get me.'

No response. He called again, starting to feel faintly ridiculous. 'Here I am, Hector. Why don't you come and get me?'

The corridors echoed, but no Demigod came stalking.

Adam began to move towards the nucleus, bitter at himself for his continuous underestimation of Hector, angry and afraid of the consequences of his own folly.

He came upon Alex by chance, surprising her in a tunnel just off the nucleus.

'Where is he?' she said, her voice lowered to no more than a whisper.

'I don't know. He was following me, and then he vanished.'

'He's planning something.'

Adam couldn't disagree. 'I only wish I knew what.'

They moved out into the nucleus. Adam said, 'I've had an idea about how we might be able to trap him, put him out of action. But first we have to know where . . .'

Alex's hand was on his arm. He glanced at her, and then followed her eyes to the far side of the nucleus. 'Keep moving,' she breathed.

The TV camera mounted high on the curving wall opposite was motoring slowly, keeping them in shot.

Hector was in the communications room. He was tracking them.

'Couldn't be better,' Adam said, hope beginning to emerge through desperation. 'Come on. We're going to the lab.'

# THIRTEEN

The lab camera motored gamely, but Adam knew that the tube was ruined and Hector would see nothing. If the robot decided to come down from the communications room they would have three minutes, four at the most.

Alex followed as Adam led the way over to the hydroponics tanks, stopping short in the open area before them.

'Give me a hand with this,' he said, and bent to lift the floor covering. Alex took the far corner and helped roll back the semi-permeable vinyl sheet that sealed over the grating of the lab floor; it was designed to permit gases through in one direction only, aided by the slightly lower air pressure in the underfloor waste pits where the hydroponics overflow was processed. The pits were over-filled and active, a result of Adam's neglect. Their condition couldn't have been better.

'Okay, stand back. Stand near the tanks.' Alex backed off, uncertain but aware of the need for fast, decisive action. Adam thrust his fingers through the grating of the first floor panel and lifted, trying to ignore the pain as the metal squeezed the soft flesh against the bone. The panel was heavy, and as it lifted he was unable to balance it. He transferred his grip from the mesh to the edge as the panel started to tilt and slide away from him, angling to fall into the pit beneath; but as it fell halfway it jammed, wedged between the two adjacent squares.

Adam lifted the next square, and the panel fell free. It hit the dark bubbling wastes edge-on and was immediately swallowed, the warm mud closing and healing behind it. The next panel fell easily into the widened gap, landing flat and floating for a moment before several hundred tiny jets fountained through its mesh and bore it down.

Two more panels and there was a sizeable hole in the lab floor, one which an active man would find difficulty in jumping across. Adam rolled back the vinyl sheet, pulling it tight at the edges in an attempt to smooth out the sag where it was unsupported.

Hector's tread could be heard as he turned into the lab corridor. It was unhurried, irresistible.

'Elephant trap,' Adam explained.

'What's an elephant?'

'Never mind. Just stay that side of the hole and get him to come towards you.' Hector was almost at the door. 'I'll get behind him in case he has second thoughts. Good luck.'

He dropped behind a lab bench as Hector appeared in the shattered doorway. The robot hesitated for a moment; he had seen Alex, and he was looking around for Adam.

Alex wanted to shout, to urge him on, but her mouth was dry and her breath was short. Hector started to move slowly, scanning around him as he went down the centre of the lab and turned to face her. Then he stepped forward, almost to the edge of the concealed pit, and stopped.

Could he have seen the tell-tale indentation of the sheet around its rim? His single eye seemed to be trained on her alone, and she didn't dare look down to reassure herself in case he followed her gaze; but still he hesitated, only inches from the illusion of security.

There was a raw metal sound from somewhere in the darkness of the lab, and the spider-robot rounded one of the benches and came trundling down. Its frame was bent and its wheels were damaged from the savage backward kick it had received from Hector, but still it obeyed him, lurching and clanking on its mis-shapen chassis as it rolled past the Demigod and on to the vinyl.

The sheet gave abruptly, collapsing in around the robot's weight and funnelling down to hit the mud. The spider struggled weakly as it turned over, supported for a moment by the outspread flooring, but then the thick waste took a firmer hold and it was pulled down, the sheet being drawn in after it.

Hector raised his eye, again brought it to bear on Alex. Then he began to move around the narrow rim of the exposed pit.

Adam hit him squarely between the shoulders, jumping high at the end of his run in an attempt to rock the Demigod far enough to tip his centre of gravity. Adam's breath was knocked from him at the impact of man on metal and as he dropped to the floor it was all he could do to roll to safety.

Hector had bent forward with the blow, and he was holding the attitude. Adam began to think with horror that he had failed, until he heard the click and whine of Hector's servos; Hector was struggling desperately to keep upright, pouring in the power to maintain the angle and prevent it from decaying any further. He couldn't step forward and, try as he might, he couldn't fall back; little by little, he was leaning closer to the edge.

Adam wanted to get to his feet and move in, give another, decisive push, but he feared the sweep of Hector's claws. The robot might catch hold of him and use him as the lever for balance that he so urgently needed.

Then the critical point was passed, and Hector began a slow tumble. He turned as he fell and landed flat, sending up a geyser of waste as it spread to receive and enfold him. He thrashed with all his limbs, reaching blindly for support or rescue in the murky soup.

'Come on, we've got time to get to the airlock.' Adam stretched out his hand to Alex, and she edged her way along the narrow strip around the pit. Hector was throwing up mud in great spurts, swimming frantically to keep his eye turret aloft and barely succeeding.

'Will the pit hold him?' she asked.

'Maybe not for long. We can only hope it's for long enough.'

James's helmet was still in the crewroom. At least he hadn't limped one-handed to his ship and made a solo escape; Hector had undoubtedly killed him after bearing him off towards the lab, but in their long flight neither Adam or Alex had seen any sign of the Captain's body. It was almost as if he'd been dismantled and packed away in the robot's transport crates – but that, of course, was a ridiculous idea.

They were suited and moving into the airlock when Adam remembered something, returning to the crewroom as fast as he could manage and going over to James's suit helmet. He lifted it anxiously, turning it to look at the radio apparatus that was moulded into the back of the shell.

There was a small box, clamped on by magnet. This was the key to the spacecraft, a sonic emitter which pulsed a coded tone through the suit radio and permitted access only to the carrier. Without it, the hatchway wouldn't open and they would be trapped on Tethys's surface, easy targets for Hector or, at best, for slow oxygen starvation.

He lifted the magnet and transferred it to his own suit radio, muttering a silent thanks that James had not thought to remove it and carry it around with him.

Then, after a nervous glance down the ramp (empty) he rejoined Alex and started the lock's cycle.

Various unpleasant thoughts haunted him as they waited for the lock to complete, thoughts of Hector finding some handhold around the rim of the pit and levering himself out, or else getting a footing on the sunken panels and using them to boost himself up. A man might well be destroyed by such a trap, but Hector was more than a man. He didn't breathe, so he couldn't drown; and as long as he had power, he could scheme and devise with an ingenuity that was fully human and pursue his plans with a body that had all the advantages of the machine.

Adam glanced at Alex, reading her with difficulty through the dark faceplate of her pressure suit helmet. She was nervous, but at no time had she lost her self-possession; Alex was far more than the fragile child he had always imagined her to be.

A light glowed by the outer door and there was a ping on their radio circuit which told them that the cycle was complete. They moved through into the hangar where the buggy and the spare sample cases were stored, crossing to the rent in the door where Adam had blown his way in during Hector's first spate of misbehaviour. Alex went through first, and then Adam stepped after on to Tethys's cold surface.

Their suit units cut in, producing heat to replace that lost by contact with the frozen ground.

'There she is,' Adam said, raising his voice to compensate for what he knew would be a poor-quality signal on Alex's receiver, 'first stage of our ticket to Earth.'

'You don't think they'll send us back here?'

'Will you *want* to come back here?'

She turned slightly as she walked, a token look at the exposed upper structure of Saturn Three. 'No,' she said decisively, 'I don't think I will.'

They walked on, the spacecraft only a couple of hundred yards ahead. Hector could never reach them now.

'Are you sure you can fly this?' Alex said.

'Of course I can. It's probably locked on automatic return, anyway. Don't forget, I'm a spacer by training and a poor man's biochemist by accident.'

She laughed, hesitantly and for the first time in many hours. He reached for the box on the outside of his helmet and activated the emitter.

The panels began to move first, lifting outwards with an ease of movement that betrayed their looseness. They drifted out in silence, carried on an expanding wave of burning fuel which split and ruptured into a number of smaller clouds and bubbles of black fire, swamping the legs of the small craft and causing it to fall into a slow tilt.

Adam pulled Alex down, tried to get them both as close to the ground as possible. Their suit units stepped up their activity as Tethys drew more heat from this closer contact. A series of smaller explosions were now ringing the craft, forcing their way out through bolted panels and weaker seams, dismantling its structure with harsh pressure from within. After no more than a fraction of a second of this internal punishment the main body of the craft hit the ground, and this additional blow ended the tenacious integrity of the hull.

The spacecraft exploded, bright fire blossoming on the snowball moon, several tons of instant debris streaking in all directions in a cometary shower. With his head half-turned Adam could see part of a complete landing-leg passing overhead, and even as this registered the ground vibrated as something ploughed into the surface close by.

Some of the wreckage was recaptured and began to fall, whilst some had been blasted so hard that it reached escape velocity and moved out to join the ice and gravel of the ring system. Adam pushed himself up to his knees, and saw that there was no trace of what had been their promise of salvation. Hope was gone, to be replaced by nothing; no fear, no desperation, no angry complaining against fate. He put his gloved hand under Alex's arm, and helped her to her feet. Saturn Three was a short walk away, and there was nowhere else to go.

They shrugged out of their pressure suits in the empty crewroom, mechanically going through basic safety and care procedures as they straightened the flexible joints and pulled out the creases in the outer layers.

'We can't run,' Alex said quietly, 'and we can't fight. What does he want from us?'

'I don't know. He's supposed to be something approaching human inside – maybe all he wants is company.' He avoided looking at Alex as he said it.

'We've been lousy hosts.'

'He's been a lousy guest. But I don't think he wants to kill us.'

'I wish I could believe that. You didn't see what he did to the Captain.'

'That was different. There was something strange between those two, ever since James started with the brain link. Everything that Hector's done since then has been to prevent us leaving, that's all.'

'That isn't how it looks to me.'

They moved down the ramp towards the nucleus. 'If he wanted to kill us, he didn't have to chase us and put us at risk. He knows the station inside out – he could have blown all the valves and decompressed us. He wouldn't have suffered, and we'd have been dead within a minute.'

'The safety doors would drop,' objected Alex.

'He could override them – but he didn't do it. He rigged the ship instead.'

The nucleus was empty. 'Where is he?' Alex whispered.

'I don't know.' Adam looked around uneasily. The open tunnels that led into the nucleus gaped with quiet and dangerous invitation. 'We'll go to the com room. We can track him from there.'

The communications room was shut down and deserted. There was evidence of Hector's presence in that the swivel chairs had been kicked aside from the console, overturning in a disordered heap against the wall to make room for the Demigod's oversized body.

Adam preselected a source for the main monitor, and hit the switch to transfer it from the mixer's memory to the monitor display. The screen came alive, but instead of showing the lab corridor as expected the scene was of the communications room itself, an infinity of Adams and Alexes looking at endless replicated images of themselves.

'Must have made a mistake,' Adam said, and punched up another source. The picture flickered momentarily, but the scene did not change. Moving aside from the main monitor controls Adam activated the smaller roving preview monitors that were grouped around it, but as each brightened it re-presented the same scene, regardless of source.

It couldn't be a simple mixer lock-up. Hector had jinxed the selectors somehow, re-routed them to deprive the com room operator of control. Adam turned to look towards the back of the room where, surely enough, the racks panels had been removed and then laid back in place without proper fixing. He started to move over for a closer look, but the reflected light of the monitors suddenly changed. Alex gave a small gasp of surprise, but when Adam turned back the screens showed nothing but flickering noise.

'What was it?' he said.

'I'm not sure. The picture changed for a moment, and then it all went off.'

'What was the picture?'

'It looked like the captain. I'm sure it was.'

'The Captain?' Adam's interest began to awaken. 'If he's still alive, then we've got a chance against Hector. As long as we can hold on until we're out of shadowlock, we can call Survey and get help.'

The intercom speaker of the station's public address system suddenly crackled and began to hum. Adam looked in surprise at the row of talkback keys that were supposedly the only trigger for this system, but they were all in the closed position.

'It's me, Major.' James's voice was flattened and depersonalised by the cheap speaker. 'As you see, I'm alive. Unlike you, I have no choice about it.'

Alex was confused. Adam shook his head, a warning against hope. He opened the general address key and said, 'What happened, Captain?'

'We came to an arrangement, Hector and I.'

'What kind of arrangement?'

'He's with me. He's under my control. There's no need to worry.'

The screens all died, and without a signal the door to the com room slid open. The corridor beyond was twilit, uninviting, and it echoed with James's voice as it carried over every intercom speaker in Saturn Three.

'Come this way,' he said, 'and you'll see what we've devised.'

The voice led them on, urging and enticing, a disembodied and spectral presence. They wanted to hold back, but they were tired of fighting and hiding; they moved on with an inner peace that was born of helpless resignation. Surely, nothing could surprise or astonish them now.

As they came to the first junction in the tunnel the walls and floor shook, the massive pressure bulkhead door at its far end slamming down. They watched with detachment as the doors banged down section by section, each drop shortening the tunnel as the apparent wave passed over them and moved on as the barriers continued to fall in the direction of the com room.

Now they were sealed into a section of the corridor. Under the grating beneath their feet a pressure-resistant foam was spreading and hardening into a dam which would back up the action of the doors. Measures designed to conserve the precious atmosphere of the station were being called into use to form a prison; they watched calmly, without enthusiasm or excitement.

'I couldn't leave you,' James said, and they turned in the direction of the voice. It came from the branching tunnel that joined their own. It was dark and open, and someone – the Captain? – was moving towards them in the shadows. 'Not,' James went on, 'when you were just on the point of accepting me as one of you.' He was drawing nearer, moving towards the slanted light that fell from the main corridor. 'You *were* going to accept me, weren't you? I know we argued, but I'm sure it's nothing that we can't settle between us. It'll be so much better this way.'

He stepped into the light. It was Hector, it was James, it was a horrifying symbiosis of both. Hector was pitted and streaked with filth from his immersion in waste, and to the filth on his chest and arms had been added an overlay of something dark and dry.

James's head was clamped firmly on to the robot's massive shoulders. The mouth was slightly open, and the lips and teeth were blackened with dried blood whilst the heavy-lidded eyes were turned upward, no pupil showing. The neck was stretched and ripped, forming a ragged edge where it met the dirty bodyshell.

Alex began to sag and Adam, holding her shoulders, could not find the strength to keep her upright; nor could he move his eyes from the macabre parody before him. He stooped, lowering her as gently as possible and falling to his knees in order to support her as she subsided to the ground. Hector began to move towards them.

# FOURTEEN

Adam awoke suddenly. The room around him was coming alive, warming and brightening as its clock setting moved into an artificial phase of day. It was an unfamiliar room, and he did not know how he had come to be in it.

As full sensation returned he became aware of a succession of minor discomforts that were beginning to make their complaints in various parts of his body. They intensified as he moved and looked about him, their low overall murmur becoming distinct individual cries of annoyance. He uncrossed his hands from his chest – an unnatural pose which suggested that he had somehow been brought here and arranged in sleep – and lifted himself on an elbow.

Now he recognised the place. It was Alex's old room, the one that they had given to James on his arrival. But why was he here?

He couldn't remember coming here, he couldn't remember being tired and falling on to the bed; nor could he remember being brought to the room by anybody else. Such ignorance was perplexing, but it led him to pay close attention to the ache that was beginning to come into focus behind his left eye, and to the bad but half-familiar taste in his mouth.

A blanker pill. Somebody had given him a blanker pill, effectively wiping out twenty-four hours or more from his memory. He'd experienced the disjointed, disoriented feeling before – back on Earth, of course, where there was so much one might want to forget, and where a temporary confusion as the gap in one's life healed and closed was far preferable to much of the unpleasantness of everyday existence.

He searched back, reaching for his last memory, trying to re-establish the continuity as quickly as possible. At first there was nothing and then, fading in from a white and featureless background, a slow replay of an exploding spacecraft. That was good, a useful point from which to begin reconstruction, but nothing came with it; the explosion simply repeated itself in his memory, bursting and burning again and again, a vivid boundary-marker for his perceptions.

The Captain; something about him, but Adam wasn't sure what. Perhaps he was alive, or injured, or dead. Adam grimaced as a further series of agonies raised a protest against his efforts to sit upright, and he started to pay closer attention to his body's dissatisfaction.

His forearms appeared to be bruised, as were his thighs above the knees; it was as if some weight had been laid across them to pin him down. His shoulders were particularly sore, and his throat was raw and dry. He'd even bitten his tongue a couple of times. Adam began to be rather glad of the blanker pill – the abuse and the pain that his injuries suggested would be better forgotten.

But what had happened? Memories of the giant Demigod, resurrected and mobile, were vague and hardly seemed to threaten at such a distance.

*I don't think he wants to kill us.*

Where, he wondered with growing unease, was Alex?

The door moved aside obediently for him, and he stepped out into the corridor. There was no sound other than the usual pump and shudder of Saturn Three's life-support systems. He wanted to run along to his own sleeping quarters, see if Alex was there; but he had to be satisfied with a stiff walk, and when he arrived the doors would not open for him. He placed his hands on and tried to push, to no effect. When he tried to knock, his hands hurt and the panel absorbed the sound. He turned away and moved towards the Central Nucleus.

The nucleus was again deserted, and he passed through and headed for the lab. One door was still peeled back, and inside the mess was just as they had left it when rhey had run to the airlock. There was a trail of dried dirt leading from the edge of the open waste pit, showing where Hector had managed to drag himself out; this, as far as Adam could see, was the only addition.

No Hector, no Alex. He moved to the edge of the pit and looked down, rubbing thoughtfully at the back of his neck.

A few seconds later he was over by the sample analysis benches, pulling the light-concentrating mirrors around to unaccustomed angles on their gooseneck mounts. He managed to position one behind his head and another before his eyes to reflect the image of the first. The mounts were never intended to work at such an angle, and they tended to pull away from him. He had to hold them in place to get the view that he wanted.

His neck was badly bruised, swelling and purple, and there was something forced under the skin that should not have been there. Adam twisted the mirror to more of an angle, but his hair was falling across and covering the area that he wanted to see. He dropped the mirror and brushed the hair aside, then tried again.

A sphincter of neat stitches held the socket in place. The skin had been shaved for about an inch all around, its exposed pinkness dragged up into little puckers by the surgical embroidery. The stitches pulled as he moved his head but the socket was firm, bone-rigid, the coloured plastic cap keeping it clear.

Last time Adam had seen the socket, it had been an

irremovable part of the Captain. Obviously this was no longer the case.

He sat back, fingers barely touching the implant, sick with a growing anger at this interference with his physical integrity. Almost as if his discovery had been awaited and noted, the lab's p.a. speaker crackled and came alive.

'Good morning, Adam.' It was James's voice. 'Did you sleep well?'

Adam looked up at the lab camera. It had turned to cover him. The access plate on its side was missing, typical of Hector's style of repair.

'What did you do to me?' Adam said, but his voice came out as little more than a croak.

'I hope you'll forgive the medication, but it was necessary, believe me. You fought me so much, and with no good reason. I'm sure the sleep was some help in getting over it.'

'Where's Alex?'

James's voice skipped on, ignoring the question. The camera tracked as Adam moved across the lab. 'Because you're probably not feeling a hundred per cent, I thought I'd give you a fairly easy programme for the day.' The lab tannoy faded as Adam stepped through the door, and a speaker in the corridor took over as the camera in a wall recess moved to take him in. 'First, we'll have to restore the damage to the lab. The open floor could be dangerous, and we want to get back to operational status as soon as possible. I notice that we're still low on samples from the PP twenty-five area on the grid since you cut your last expedition short. We'll get that shortfall made up as soon as we can spare you for a few hours. In the meantime, since we'll be doing work on the hydroponics waste pits we might as well catch up on general maintenance. Base computer tells me they need far more frequent attention than you seem to have been giving them lately.'

The com room was empty. The screens all changed abruptly as he entered, a dozen Adams standing alone in the doorways of a dozen com rooms.

He moved to the console, becoming images within images as the com room camera moved with him. The mixer panel was lit but unresponsive, more or less as he had expected. He looked up. James's voice was still chattering from the corner speaker, lining up an endless series of petty tasks for Adam.

'What are you trying to put into my head?' he demanded.

'Put in?' The Captin's voice seemed to contain a note of genuine surprise. 'I don't think you understand. As far as we know, the brain link is a one-way contact. Of course, that may not be the case; but we'll have plenty of time to experiment later. In the meantime, I'm quite happy to be taking out. I find your mind so interesting. And you have such an abundance of energy to go with it; quite remarkable. For your age, that is.'

'Where's Alex?'

'Please be patient, Adam. Any questions you want to ask will be answered when the time comes.'

'What have you done with her?'

'I've asked you to be patient. Much as I'd like to continue this discussion, I have some pressing business to attend to. Saturn Three is emerging from eclipse with regard to the Survey platform, and it seems they wish to speak to us. Excuse me for a moment.'

The Survey platform? Adam stood for a moment as if unable to believe his ears, and then snapped out of the dream state and looked around. Ignoring the aches that the activity caused he righted one of the discarded swivel chairs and pulled it over to the console, sliding into it and readying himself for the first bleep of the Survey contact signal.

'This is Survey Nineteen. Come in Saturn Three.' The voice was distant and harsh, the delivery casual but precise. 'Come in Saturn Three. Shake out the sack and get your butts to the com room.'

'Hello, Nineteen, this is Saturn Three. You won't believe how . . .' Adam's voice tailed off, and his momentary surge of joy evaporated. The pick-up microphone was dead and another voice indistinguishable from his own was broadcasting a reply.

'Saturn Three,' acknowledged the voice that was not Adam's. 'Receiving you, Survey.'

'Routine check on shadowlock emergence. Won't keep you any time at all, Three.'

'Don't worry about it. Nice to hear another voice once in a while.'

'Come off it, Three. Everybody up here knows how much you like your privacy. Can't say I blame you, either. How's our favourite Spaceborn?'

There was a laugh in the voice of the not-Adam. 'She's fine, never been better.'

'She anywhere around?'

'Right next to me. You want a word?'

'Wouldn't miss a chance like that. Put her on.'

There was a pause, a shuffling. Then a voice that was either Alex or a perfect imitation said, 'Hello out there.'

'Hello to you. How's the old man treating you?'

'No problem. Any time he gets frisky, I hide his walking frame. What's new with the Survey?'

'May be some good news from Titan next month, we're all keeping our fingers crossed.'

'Sure.' Not-Alex sounded like she'd heard it all before. 'There's *always* going to be good news from Titan next month. I'll believe it when I see it.'

'You could surprise us yet. How are you getting on with that Demigod unit we dropped you?'

'Best thing you ever did for us, no complaints at all. You've no scandal for us?'

'Scandal? Clean-living boys like us? No chance. We had a monkey name of Benson space himself last month. Don't think you knew him, he was fresh out from Earth. Course failure. We never found the body.'

For a moment there was radio silence. Then, when the simulacrum of Adam's voice returned, it was strangely devoid of its earlier air of bonhomie.

'We've nothing else to tell you,' he said. 'Any urgent messages?'

'Not this time around.' The contact man on the platform was obviously puzzled by the sudden switch in mood, but he did not pry. 'Have to love you and leave you, Three, I've got Enceladus coming up in four and a half minutes.'

'Saturn Three out. Nice to talk to you.'

'And to you. Until next time.'

Adam sat back in the swivel chair, eyes focused on nowhere, his hand lightly touching the soreness of the implant at the back of his head. Had he really expected that Hector would overlook their one line of communication with the platform? Logic said no, but still Adam had leapt at what he thought was the opportunity. The predisposition of the human spirit towards hope, he reflected, was immense and inexplicable.

'Now, Adam, I think we can proceed.' The voice was back to James, and had become businesslike again. 'Please make your way to the laboratory, then we can get started.'

Adam did not react, but stared ahead as if he had not heard. The com room door abruptly slid open, as if to encourage him.

'Please, Adam. I'd prefer not to have to force you.'

Adam turned his head slowly, looked at the door without interest. Force me, you bastard, he thought. You want anything from me, you can force me.

The door zipped closed, almost in a gesture of impatience. 'Listen, Adam. You could starve, you could fry, you could freeze. I could do any of this to you if you don't co-operate. And whatever happens to you will also affect Alex.'

The door opened again, his second chance, and this time he moved. The voice moved with him, transferring to a corridor speaker. Hector had become more than a robot, he had somehow managed to soak himself into the very fabric of the station. Saturn Three had become one vast and all-enveloping extension of the Demigod's perceptions and personality.

'That's good. I'm glad you've decided to see sense. This way we can come to the best working arrangement.'

Alex emerged into the nucleus at the same moment as Adam, and they fell together in relief, James/Hector ignored for the moment.

'Hurry along, please,' said the tannoy voice testily.

'He was using your voice,' Alex whispered into Adam's ear. 'I thought I was going mad.'

As he held her he lifted his hand, pushing her long hair aside and hoping that she wouldn't realise what he was doing. His fingers brushed the downy furrow at the back of her neck, but there was no sign of the robot's rough surgery. Confusion began to edge against relief, and she said, 'What are you doing?'

'Go along to the lab,' he said, his voice deliberately low. 'I'll join you in just a minute.'

'Go in on my own? Adam, I can't.'

'You have to.' He turned his head aside, and her eyes widened as she saw the implant and the mistreated flesh around it. 'I need you to keep him occupied so he won't be able to watch me.'

She shook her head, and Adam gave her a squeeze of encouragement. 'You can do it. When you're around he doesn't seem to be able to see anything else.'

He kissed her once, and then moved away. She stayed in the nucleus, looking after him; he turned, gave her a smile of confident assurance, and then walked on in the direction of the ramp and the upper nucleus.

Hector had tidied himself up for her. The blood and the dirt were gone, and the golden curves of his body-shell had been polished to a high brilliance. One could almost have believed him to be a tall and superhuman figure with his armour moulded into the shape of a musculature and his human stance, but as a subtitute for a man he was incomplete and unconvincing. The utilitarian swivels and servos of his arms and hands gave him away, as did the turret and anglepoise mechanism that served him for a head.

Perhaps it had bothered him once; it didn't seem to bother him now. He'd obviously found some better salve for his ego. The turret came around to bear on her, and then dodged slightly to either side, looking for Adam to follow through the gap in the lab door.

'You called me,' she said quickly, hoping to capture his attention before he could become curious. 'Here I am.'

'So you are.' The voice was Adam's. The sensor moved to her and stayed on her. 'May I say how beautiful you are looking today. Please, come forward where I can see you better.'

'What now, Hector?' she said resignedly as she walked down the centre of the lab. The robot was near the open pit at its far end, ready to supervise the retrieval of the covers and their subsequent replacement. 'What are you going to do with us?'

'That name, please. I never liked it.' The right-hand

claw came up and made a derisory little gesture, a throwaway of nothing. The voice might be Adam's, but the personality beneath seemed still to belong more to the Captain.

'I thought he was supposed to be some kind of hero.'

'For a time. But in the end he was a loser. He was killed by Achilles, and his body was dragged around the walls of Troy behind his murderer's chariot. Is that a worthwhile end for a hero? To be thrown to the dogs to be mauled? No, I don't think Hector's a very good name at all.'

'What would you prefer?'

'Adam. I think Adam will be considerably more appropriate, don't you?'

'Stop it!' she said, shocked by the Demigod's presumption. 'And stop using his voice!'

'Not *his* voice. *My* voice. Or at least, it soon will be. For the moment I'll admit that I'm only borrowing it, but the time will soon come when I take it over completely. You see, we're brainlinked, Adam and I. And when he's a drained and empty shell, and I speak to you with his voice and share all your secrets with you – well, you may reject me now, but I think you'll have to accept me when the time comes.'

'No. Never!'

'I understand your feelings, believe me. The Captain has a lot to answer for – I know he presented me in the worst possible light, but the choice wasn't mine, and try as I might I know I can never overcome that with you. But I want you to consider this. When I came to Saturn Three I was blank, unrecorded, nothing in my mind apart from what was put there through the link. You can't hold me responsible for what I did, Alex, surely you must understand that. My body, Adam's body – they're just vehicles for intellects and concepts.

And when his intelligence fully inhabits my mind, drives out the Captain and everything bad that he put in – won't you love me exactly as you love him now?'

'No,' she said.

'Then you'll condemn him to an agony he doesn't deserve. Because it will be him, Alex, walking and talking in this metal body. He'll give you all the consideration and affection he ever did. Reject him then and it will be no different from rejecting him now.'

'You really expect me to believe all this?'

'But why should I lie to you? I need you to understand. And think about this, Alex; he's so much older than you, and his body can't hold together forever. And when it comes to a choice of having him survive in me or lose him as he is, I think you can see the only sensible course to take. His memories will be continuous, his feelings will persist as before. All I ask is that I should be allowed to share.'

'This is monstrous. I don't believe you can have any idea of what it is you're suggesting.'

'Monstrous?' said not-Adam, with apparent sadness. 'Yes, I suppose it is. But it's the only option that's been given to me.'

There was a noise behind Alex, and she saw that the robot suddenly looked beyond her to the lab door. Turning, she saw with relief that it was Adam.

'You're late, Adam,' the Demigod said. Adam didn't move into the lab, but hesitated in the shattered doorway with one hand on the frame. 'Hear this now and remember it. Don't ever be late again when I call you.'

'You don't call anything around here, Hector.' As Adam stepped forward in his own time Alex noticed that he'd changed his clothes. He looked untidy, as if the uniform jumpsuit was a couple of sizes too large for him, but he walked down the lab with an air of confident command. 'And you will call me Major. I'm the base commander, and you'll do well to bear that in mind.'

The sensor lowered a little, took in the rank flashes on Adam's shoulders. Then, as if shaking off some short-lived preoccupation, it reared up again.

'Please don't be awkward, Adam. I admit I expected something like this, but it will do you no good at all.' Hector's left hand came up, and Alex saw for the first time that it held the jack-connection probe that was the transmitting component of the brain link, delicately angled between opposable claws.

'Adam, don't go near him!' she said urgently, but Adam was already past her and he waved her back so savagely that she dared not argue.

'Considering your attitude,' Hector went on, 'this may be a suitable opportunity to find out whether brain link programming can actually be a two-way affair. I've made certain modifications in the wave transmitter so that it can now act as a partial resonator. It will be useful to have some more definite assurance of your obedience.'

'Keep talking, Captain.' Hector, who was about to do just that, was pulled up short by the name. 'Yes,' Adam went on, 'that's who you really are. That's who you'll always be.' He arrived at the edge of the pit and stopped, just out of the robot's reach. 'No escape from him, Hector. He's there in your head, and that's where he'll stay.'

'We'll have to see,' Hector said calmly. 'Come here.' Adam smiled.

'Please,' Alex began, unable to watch this wary game with danger in silence, but Adam cut her off with a side-ways glance. When his eyes returned to Hector, he was smiling again.

'No deal, Captain,' he said. 'Sorry.'

'I don't wish to damage you,' Hector warned, stepping forward and reaching for Adam with his right claw. 'Don't make this more difficult.'

Adam didn't pull back, but he flinched as the claw took a grip on his shoulder. It squeezed the muscle and sinew above his collar-bone, fitting directly into a pattern of bruises which betrayed the fact that Adam had been held in exactly the same way at some time in the recent past. Hector tried to turn him, but he set his teeth and resisted so that the robot had to take a sideways step to reach around with the probe.

'It's not your fault, Hector,' Adam said. The robot was having difficulty; he couldn't hold the probe and remove the plastic cap with the same claw, but the other was holding Adam steady.

Adam's hand was on Hector's shoulder, seeming to pull him in close rather than fend him off. With the other hand he took hold of the supporting frame of the Demigod's outstretched arm, and without warning hoisted himself off the floor.

Hector staggered forward as he became unexpectedly top-heavy, but he corrected with a step that banged his metal knee-joint hard into Adam's leg. They were inches away from the lip of the waste pit, but Hector was taking Adam's extra weight with no trouble.

Adam held his grip on arm and bodyshell, and tried to climb. The claw on his shoulder pushed him down but Hector was beginning to wobble, unable to make adequate compensation for the unexpected shifts of balance; now Adam had got a grip on the turret housing, and Hector began to panic. He was was leaning forward at an increasing angle, servos screaming to resist, and Adam was, slowly but surely, toppling him towards the pit.

Alex wanted to cry out, to beg Adam to stop, but she

knew that it would be futile. Even if Hector could be tipped once more into the waste pit the deep silt would not hold him for long, as they already knew; but there was a real danger that Adam might be drowned, or else injured by the robot's threshing about.

Hector managed to force Adam away, the claw on his shoulder biting deep to rip him free and throw him into the pit. Adam swung out and saw the floor pass from beneath him but he got a hold with both hands on Hector's outstretched arm, and when the claw released he hung on.

The Demigod was taken by surprise. As the claw had opened his servos had cut to prevent him falling backwards as Adam's weight was unloaded, but it didn't happen. Adam clung to the limb, feeling through it that the whole of the robot's body was falling towards him and had passed the point of recovery. Only then did he let go, and man and machine fell together towards the slime.

Alex ran to the edge and looked down, hoping she could find some way to reach Adam and get him clear before he could be hurt. Hector had vanished beneath the surface of the mud almost immediately but there was a heaving and boiling that indicated his efforts to get back to the surface. Adam was swimming, irrationally tearing at his upper clothing to be free of it.

'I'll get a cable or something,' she shouted to him.

'No, Alex, please,' he gasped. 'Get out of the lab!'

His tunic split as he turned over in the thick mud. He managed to get his arm out of one of the sleeves. There was blood on his shoulder where the robot's grasp had broken the skin, and Alex could see the reason for the poor fit of the uniform; Adam was wearing a makeshift harness of crossed equipment belts. Both belts had a number of the highly explosive red quarry grenades fastened to them, and a continuous run of wire appeared to link all the grenades together.

'No, Adam,' she cried, 'no!'

'For the last time, get out of the lab!'

Something broke the surface only a couple of feet away from him. It was Hector's eye apparatus, and it shook itself free of obscuring filth before swinging around and fixing on him. A claw erupted through the mud and made a grab, but missed. Adam didn't wait for another opportunity, but dived down towards where he now knew Hector to be.

Alex was thrown back as the section of floor on which she was standing lifted at an angle. The open pit before her was an overflowing geyser, a flood of waste hurling itself at the ceiling of the lab and raining down on to everything around her. Every floor section had buckled at the pressure from beneath, but the roar of the multiple explosion was softened, somehow muted by the sluggish reaction of its sloppy medium.

The floor dropped more or less back into place but the rain continued for several seconds, splattering and peppering every exposed surface with fragmented wet pellets. The silence that followed was absolute, until the lifeline sounds of Saturn Three began to filter back into her awareness.

She crawled to the edge of the pit and looked in, afraid of what she might see but unable to resist. The pit was empty, excavated right down to the riveted plates at its base. Of Adam and Hector there was no sign at all.

# FIFTEEN

It was difficult to know what to do. There was a dark emptiness inside that she knew would eventually fill and become grief, but until that time her calmness was almost an embarrassment to her. She showered to rid herself of the covering of slurry that she'd acquired in the lab explosion and dressed in a clean jumpsuit. Then, with her hair still damp, she went through to the general living quarters and sat on a lay-low.

It wouldn't matter that she had no control over the station's communications. When no acknowledgement was received on the platform to the information scans that were sent with great frequency to make the most of their time out of shadowlock, then an investigation would surely follow. She'd be lifted, and she'd be sent – where?

Alex didn't want to stay in Saturn Three, although the strength of Adam's presence in its corridors and work areas would make the leaving more difficult. But she could take Adam's memory with her, leaving the ghosts of Hector and James to prowl the tunnels alone. This, and the prospective realisation of what might prove to be a dangerous dream, would make the departure a little less hard to bear.

She eased back on the lay-low, and gazed despondently at the ceiling. The area's camera was trained on her.

It was a coincidence that she should choose to sit directly in the line of the camera's last angle. It shouldn't bother her, but it did. She decided to move to another lay-low.

The camera tracked her as she crossed the room.

She stopped, and the camera stopped. She began to shake her head in slow disbelief. Hector couldn't have survived; even if his body had not been mangled and ruined by the clutch of grenades his brain tissue would never have withstood the blast.

'Hector?' she said. 'Is that you?'

When she took a step towards the door the camera stayed immobile, as if the intelligence behind it was sheepishly hoping to compensate for its discovery with a period of deceptive stillness.

She checked the com room but there was nobody, the only sign that it had even been visited in the last few hours being the swivel chair that Adam had dragged over to the console. This gave her a momentary elation which was quickly beaten down by rationality; if she was so sure that Hector had been destroyed there was no possible hope for Adam, pressing himself and his deadly harness close to the robot's chest.

The corridor camera moved with her as she went towards the sleeping quarters they had shared. There was nobody there, no sign of interference with the station commander's spy-eye console. The p.a. speaker was live, but there was no sound other than a low hiss coming from it; and though she spoke out loud, calling to Hector and Adam a number of times, there was no hint of a reply.

Steadily and with full self-control she set out to check out the complete corridor complex of the station. It was not so large and rambling that she found any part of it unfamiliar, but never before had she set out to cover it in one continuous tour, and certainly there were some tunnels leading to disused quarters that she'd never had occasion to visit more than once or twice. She went into each room, checked every possible compartment, and even kept an eye on the grating underfoot as she moved from one place to another. Sometimes cameras motored to follow her, but mostly they were still. It was as if the directing intellect behind them lacked the energy to manage more than one shot every few minutes, but whose intellect, she wondered, and where? Each turn and intersection betrayed nothing more remarkable than yet more tunnel and corridor spaces – no broken metal carcase pulling itself along, no torn and bloody Adam. She'd been there, only a few yards from the explosion. She'd crawled to the edge of the pit and looked over, and there had been nothing. Adam had probably been dissolved by the close heat of the grenades, and Hector had almost certainly been ripped into a shrapnel too fragmentary ever to be re-assembled.

Before the lab door, she hesitated. Of all the station, the two miles or more of convoluted and winding corridor, this was the one section that she had repeatedly avoided. When she had walked out she had been upright and without tears, a promise of strength that she had made in silence to Adam. She wasn't sure that she could do so well a second time. But then the wall camera had made a weak attempt to turn and cover her, and this had aided her resolve. She stepped through the peeled-back door.

The lab was as she had left it. Most of the benches were collapsed or overturned, and some of the tanks were split and empty. The lighting was patchy and uneven due to the spattering of mud that had been thrown across most of the panels; in fact there was little that had escaped such a coating, the far-flung streaks of mud radiating outwards from the open pit and stencilled into a star-pattern on the floor where sufficiently large objects had intercepted the rain. The hydroponics tanks were ruined, close as they had been to the explosion, but the experiments could be restarted by the next crew –

assuming that Survey didn't decide to close the station down. Until then, the loss of the minor oxygen output of the tanks would be insignificant.

After a few minutes of walking around and looking at the floor she came across a twist of metal that was almost recognisable. She picked it up carefully and found that it was a part of one of the robot's claws, bent and compressed out of shape. After this find her luck seemed to improve and she came across a number of identifiable components – none, thankfully, that could be ascribed to Adam, but a search of perhaps an hour yielded a respectable heap of scrap which she piled in the middle of the lab floor. When she decided that she'd amassed enough she returned and began to sort through the pieces. She almost enjoyed the dull, undemanding work. It allowed her mind an escape from the realities of the moment, realities to which she had not yet decided her reaction. There would be grief, unhappiness, self-reproach; but for the present they held themselves back, and allowed mere preoccupation to take their place.

Like a palaeontologist she laid out the fragments, mapping the outline of Hector's body and filling in the gaps with her imagination. There was a claw here, a loop of tubing there, even a complete section of the turret mechanism. The largest pieces of all were curled shreds of the golden body shell and there, in their midst, was the prize; a chunk of glass crystal with embedded wires which could only be from the Demigod's ruined braincase.

Hector had been blown right apart, there could be no doubt about it. The varied evidence before her showed that no single part of the robot had remained intact, no crippled shell that could be hiding in some unchecked corner and gathering strength to reach for her again. The signs and motions of surveillance could be no more than shadows of the Demigod's occupying dominance of the internal systems of Saturn Three.

The lab camera was on her again, she noted with irritation. She found an upturned box and dragged it over, stepping on to it and reaching for the lens; the camera tried to pull away, but she easily overcame the servo mechanism and held the apparatus still with one hand whilst reaching for the focus ring with the other. She gave the ring a sharp twist to its fullest extent, defocusing the tube and effectively blinding the camera. The ring started to rotate weakly back to its former position, but she gave it another twist and this time it stayed in place.

Alex wasn't afraid; it was as if Hector had drained off his rightful supply of terror, and these feeble after-images of menace could raise no response from her. The robot had claimed that the body was no more than a vehicle for the intellect, a medium through which the mind could express itself. In this way the Demigod had tried to claim some right to considerations of humanity, and had even supposed that he might, by becoming a copy of Adam's intellect and destroying the original, gain access to her affections. Was it possible that the reverse had somehow happened and that Hector, by imposing his will on the station computer to take control of its subsidiary systems, had forced the machine into a model of himself?

Only now did the fear begin to re-awaken. When acknowledgement was sought by Survey it might be given spontaneously by the computer, urged by Hector's personality within it. Rescue could be delayed, or it might never come. Deprived of her immediate company, the Demigod would perhaps be content to watch her, an eternal and insatiable voyeur, resigned to impotence but too stubborn to let go.

The focus ring was pulling itself back, turning in millimetre bursts. She could cut the power to the computer, but Saturn Three's life-support would cease functioning immediately. There would be emergency lighting, and probably enough air in the station to last her for many months before it started to grow stale; but after only a few minutes the temperature of the buried structure would start to drop. Inside a pressure suit she could last for a few days, replacing the power packs with spares as they ran out, but in the end she would be forced to restore power to the computer in order to survive. And when the computer came back there Hector would be, watching.

'You won't leave me alone, will you?' she said, her voice sounding unnaturally loud in the stillness of the lab. 'You're beaten and you know it, but you won't let go.'

The camera stared, unable to respond. The p.a. speaker crackled in a snowstorm of white noise, but the formless sound shaped into no message.

Then it turned, inching slowly and angling away, tilting downward in an attitude of dejection. At first this is how she interpreted the move, before she overcame this anthropomorphic tendency and looked around to see what the camera might be pointing at.

The VDU was on its side, mud-covered and cemented where it had fallen. The connecting cables were out of the wall socket and coiled into loose snakes behind the unit.

'You want me to plug it in? Is that what you want?' Of course, the computer/Hector had no way of answering. With a slight smile she kicked the box aside and walked out of the lab.

There was a degree of satisfaction in being able, at

last, to deny something to the Demigod which he could not reach out and angrily take. That had been his inheritance from James, an uncontrolled and egotistical impatience. She arrived back in general quarters and the camera was waiting, trained on the open end of the tunnel as she emerged.

She drew a glass of amber juice and sat down. The camera followed, thirsty for vicarious activity. She could go round the base and defocus each camera in turn, but Hector would eventually realign them. Probably she would have to smash the units to blind him, trap him in the petty sensations of life-support feedback. She hesitated over this course of action, not knowing what his reaction might be to such irrevocable antagonism. After all, he inhabited the station around her, and Alex's safety was only guaranteed as long as his regard for her was greater than his resentment.

At the moment it seemed that she had some small amount of dominance over him. She could hurt him, but she would have to be careful; she couldn't risk him spoiling her chances of rescue, and she had no real idea of the extent of his abilities. So far he had opened no doors, slammed down no bulkhead seals, issued no directives. That did not, unfortunately, assure her that he was incapable; underestimating Hector had caused their downfall a number of times now. As a strategy, it was due for a change. Resignedly she set down the amber juice and returned to the lab.

She was theoretically his prisoner, but she had the power to offend and wound him. Some kind of stalemate could be agreed on that basis.

She righted the VDU and cleaned the obscuring crust from its screen and keyboard before plugging it in. It warmed immediately and the line-scan came in after only a few moments. She switched to computer display.

THANK YOU

The first response surprised her. It didn't sound like Hector at all.

'Can you hear me if I speak out loud?'

YES

'Okay. Now, I've got some idea of where you are and how you got there. I know you've got control of the cameras and not much more.' The unit didn't react, so she went on, 'I can wreck the cameras or burn them out. Either way you'll be blind. I'll do it if you don't leave me alone. Do you understand that?' No response; so she raised her voice. 'I said do you understand that, Hector?'

NOT HECTOR

She suspected some deceit. The base computer was no more than a standard data processing unit without a personality of its own; any original thought or direction would have to be superimposed from without, and Hector had been the only organism who might have been capable of such influence. The pit of frustrated snakes that had comprised the darker side of James's nature had found full expression in the Demigod, and now it seemed that they lived on, a howling pack of furies that needed no flesh for their embodiment.

'I don't believe you.'

NOT HECTOR

'Then, who are you?'

ALEX REMEMBER . . . ALEX BELIEVE

'Remember what? And what am I supposed to believe?' Nothing happened, and so she said, 'I'm not going to waste my time. I'm going to cut the VDU.'

PLEASE

She had already reached out for the cut-off switch, but at the flat, toneless plea she hesitated and finally lowered her hand.

ALEX BELIEVE . . . WE LOVE YOU . . . ALEX REMEMBER

'We? What do you mean, we? Who are you?'

NOT HECTOR

'You must be Hector. You couldn't be anyone else.'

ADAM

Alex stared at the screen for a long moment. Then she slowly reached for the cut-off.

PLEASE

'You're lying to me. It won't work.'

NOT LIE

'Adam's dead. Don't think you can get around me by cheapening his memory.'

ADAM LIVE IN HECTOR . . . HECTOR MAKE WAY FOR ADAM SO ALEX BELIEVE . . . ALEX REMEMBER ADAM

She was angry, and more than a little frightened. 'What are you trying to do to me? Haven't you done enough already? Are you going to keep me here and play with me forever?'

ALEX SAFE . . . ADAM CALL SURVEY

'What? What was that?'

ADAM CALL SURVEY . . . ALEX SEE EARTH . . . REMEMBER ADAM

She sat in silence, appalled at the scope of Hector's ingenuity and amazed by his insensitivity. The words stayed to brighten the screen for several seconds, and then they slowly faded.

'It won't work,' she said again. 'You think you'll persuade me to stay by pretending there's something of him left in you. Forget it, Hector.'

NOT STAY . . . ALEX SEE EARTH

'I said forget it.'

I LOVED YOU

There was a pause for a few moments and then:

## WE ALL DID

Without warning the screen darkened and died as the power supply was cut. Alex flicked the power switch but it had no effect.

She stepped back from the VDU, but the lab camera did not track. When she pulled her box back and twisted the lens out of focus it made no effort to return.

How could he lead her along and then desert her? What strategy of cruelty was this, that he should defy annihilation to pester her with doubt? What could he possibly hope to gain?

Everything had been clear-cut before. She could have sustained the loss of Adam, knowing that he had died as he had lived, purposefully and with determination; but this twilight of uncertainty that Hector was creating pulled at her, destroying her composure and undermining her self-control. Of course she didn't believe the Demigod's subterfuge, but how could she be completely sure? How could she know that she wouldn't wound and offened some vestigial trace of Adam's personality, translated and replicated through the brainlink and the station computer? It didn't matter that the trace was no more than a phased recording in the memory of a machine, for the Demigod's argument came back to her with a conviction that was now far less easy to overcome. If the body was no more than a vehicle for the intellect, perhaps Adam lived on as long as his thoughts and ideas retained their coherence, whatever the medium.

Alex was startled as the tannoy spattered and came to life. 'Saturn Three,' it said, 'We understand you have a problem. Do you read?'

The corridors echoed as every speaker in the base carried the same message. 'Saturn Three, this is Survey. I repeat, is there a problem?'

She ran to the com room. All the screens were lit and

showing their usual views of the work areas and corridors. 'Last call, Saturn Three,' the voice from the platform was saying as she reached the console. 'Last call and then we come and bale you out. You'd better have a good reason for this, Three.'

'Saturn Three here,' she said breathlessly, not really expecting to be heard, but then she was surprised when the voice replied immediately.

'Hi, Spaceborn. The Major there?'

'No. No, he's . . . not here.'

'Got a call from him less than four minutes ago, really weak signal. Some kind of distress code, but we couldn't make out what.'

'That's right. We've been having some trouble with the robot you sent us.'

'Sounds like we'll have to dig out the guarantee. You want to enter for a replacement?'

'It's more serious than that. I think somebody ought to come down.'

There was a silence at the other end of the link which implied a hurried conference. Then: 'Better put the Major on.'

'I'm sorry, I can't. The Major's . . . hurt.'

'Is that part of the trouble?'

'Yes. It's really too complicated to explain.'

'Okay, we're getting a cruiser on its way to you. Can you hold on for a couple of hours?'

'I think so. But please, before you go . . . will you tell me something?'

'Make it fast.'

'When you got the call, was it the Major who spoke to you? Or was it just the code?'

'It was him, all right. I spent three years alongside that monkey on the Venus slingshot. I'd know him anywhere.'

'I see. Thanks.'

'Trade you, Spaceborn.'

What did he mean by that? 'I'm sorry?'

'Trade you information, something I didn't understand. The Major said – well it sounded like, "look after Alex". You got anybody called Alex down there?'

'No,' she said. 'I don't know who he could have meant.'

# SIXTEEN

The weeks spent on the Orion shuttle between the Saturn platform and Earth were never more than vaguely pleasant for the travellers on board. Those making their first trip were naturally excited by the novelty of their circumstances, but even this mood was eventually worn down by the killing routine of mild amusement. The movies, the magazines, the long-drawn-out dinners and the drunken jags, the blue dreams and the bed-hopping – all of the pastimes devised by the bored voyagers were never any more than the term implied, a means of speeding up the slow passage of the hours. After a while the fun became yet another routine, a mechanical process of enjoyment to be gone through as a matter of form.

Such travel, consisting of isolation in a void with no direct control over one's progress and no satisfying feedback from the changing of one's surroundings, is surely one of the least rewarding activities made possible by technological advance. Departure and arrival are the only significant realities; in between the two the continuity of existence is suspended, and any action taken during that period of not-time is leached of any worth. Books read are instantly forgotten, relationships formed and promises made are unreal in retrospect. There was a certain desperation evident under the superficially light-hearted mood of the Orion passengers. Only the crew seemed to be free of it, occasionally glimpsed like some rare species as they moved about the decks from one roped-off private burrow to another. Their continuity was somehow intact; they were more than *in transit*, they were actually alive. They kept their own society. They managed to make the passengers feel even more estranged.

The Orion was a rambling structure, space-assembled and designed exclusively for long hops between orbiting platforms. Of all the passengers only Alex seemed to find its environment comfortable, for it was hardly different from any of the places in which she had lived. If anything it was more spacious, and she derived an additional sense of awe from walking around the full circle of the promenade deck and looking out of the screens at the seemingly endless emptiness that surrounded the shuttle. She usually found herself alone on the deck, and this was one of the reasons for her frequent and prolonged visits. People, large numbers of them with over-loud voices and unattractive habits, were a source of extreme discomfort to her. She was gradually learning how to handle them – mainly by finding ways of persuading them to leave her alone – but it was a slow and depressing business. She'd not yet had any problem with sexual overtures; it wasn't that none had been made towards her, but with civilian passengers she was able to pull back into the shell of her military status, and she was fortunate in outranking the few Survey monkeys who were making the trip back home.

No doubt she would get used to being a Major. Her grasp of the hierarchy of the Survey was not very good, but it had at least been sufficient for her to be able to put the case for her promotion back on the platform. How, she had demanded, could they ignore her experience and close knowledge of the workings of Saturn Three as they worked on plans to restore its operations? But, they had said, their aim was to rationalise the station. They wouldn't need *any* ranking staff, experienced or otherwise. And then she had made her carefully-thought-out proposal.

Sometimes she would absently slip her hand under her hair, and lightly touch the implant at the back of her neck. Part of her mind would always resent its presence, even though its installation had been her own idea. She'd done well in the tests, scoring high on stability and control and convincing even the most sceptical of the members of the Survey Forward Planning Board that she should be engaged to programme the new Saturn Three Demigod.

She had never told them the real reason. They would laugh at her worries, dismiss her ideas. Instead she had transformed her determination into a reasonable facsimile of loyal enthusiasm, her very thoughts on offer for the benefit of the Survey.

There was a clear tone, and some kind of an announcement. Earth was only a few hours away – or, at least, that was when they would rendezvous with the orbiting platform from which they would be taxied to re-entry. Although she was alone on the observation deck Alex could sense the shiver of excitement that was passing through the ship, a re-awakening of the senses at the prospect of resuming interrupted lives.

She would hate it, she knew. Adam had told her so often enough, and she had come to believe it. Even so, he had been prepared to accompany her, to leave the unhurried peace of Tethys that he had loved so much. Now he need never leave, and the sacrifice need never be made. He had become part of the very fabric of the station, his mind holding together within the neural lifelines of the base in the same way that her own had been re-drawn in the Demigod.

Adam and Alex, together again in Saturn Three.
Forever.